THE RED RED DRAGON

LYNNE REID BANKS

ILLUSTRATED BY **KRISTINA KISTER**

WALKER
BOOKS

For Gillon,
my very own full-grown, without whose brilliant think-space
my red dragon could never have flown.

L.R.B.

First published 2022 by Walker Books Ltd
87 Vauxhall Walk, London SE11 5HJ

2 4 6 8 10 9 7 5 3 1

Text © 2022 Lynne Reid Banks
Illustrations © 2022 Kristina Kister

The right of Lynne Reid Banks to be identified as author of
this work has been asserted in accordance with the
Copyright, Designs and Patents Act 1988

This book has been typeset in Stempel Schneidler

Printed and bound by CPI Group (UK) Ltd, Croydon CR0 4YY

British Library Cataloguing in Publication Data:
a catalogue record for this book is available from the British Library

ISBN 978-1-5295-0779-9

www.walker.co.uk

"Come not between the dragon and his wrath."

William Shakespeare
(King Lear, Act I Scene 1)

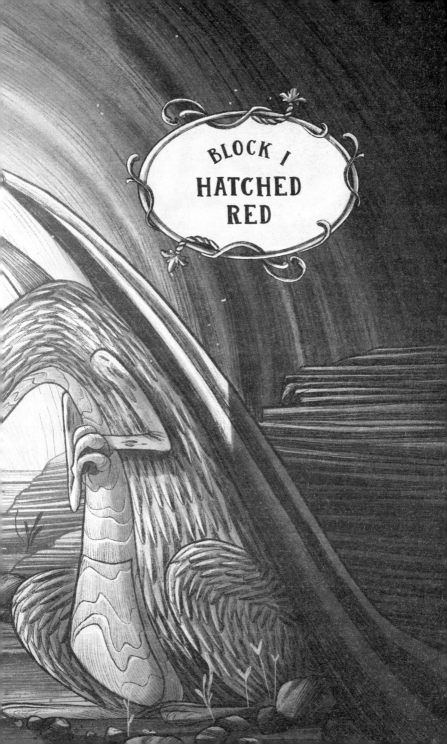

CHAPTER 1

When he was first hatched, his parents had no reason
to suspect that he wasn't a perfectly ordinary –
though, for them, precious and special – tiny dragon.

As the thick white shell of his egg fell apart and
revealed him curled inside, gazing up at them with
blinking eyes and breathing out just the faintest trickle
of infant smoke, his mag and dag bent their long necks
and nuzzled him, the way dragons do, and licked
him with their forked tongues. He was smooth and
hairless, soft, cool and cuddly as a dragon hatchling
should be.

His colour?

A sort of beige, which is the colour most hatchling
dragons are before they become brown or green or
black. If there was the faintest tinge of pinkness to his
skin, they put it down to reflected firelight. What else?

Before long he was able to stand on his strong little

hind legs and jump about their cave with the help of his tail, not yet full-length, with the point on the end of it still quite soft. He sometimes curled it into his mouth to chew when he was dropping off to sleep.

His front paws began to sprout claws, and his forehead two knobbly horns. For his parents, these were exciting stages of their son's growth, and they blew thick white smoke at each other to celebrate. Dragon smoke, of course, is quite free of any nasty stuff due to the filter in their throats. The filter doesn't work as well on black smoke, but this family didn't blow any of *that* kind.

The development of the young dragon's wings, which had been all scrunched up like fine crumpled leather when he was first hatched, was even more exciting. It meant he was beginning to grow from a hatchling into a mumbo, as young dragons are called.

Shortly after, he spoke his first *words*.

There was still a certain sense of wonderment among dragons when their young ones began to use words that, for untold lights and darks, dragons had not had. While all dragons tried not to think about the terrible time before the Great Ridding, they had a dragonlore back-think of an age when uprights ruled, and only they among the living things of the world had the ability to communicate in *language*.

Now dragons could talk.

How this had come to pass, none of them were certain, but it had something to do with a cataclysmic event many, many dragon hatchings and life-overs ago – one that had changed dragons' think-spaces and throats and made it possible for them to speak. This event was referred to as the Ear Breaker, from which the world had emerged as a much emptier place, but one in which dragons could come into their own.

Other events that had contributed were seldom spoken of, except in occasional heads-togethers among the wiser dragons, who thought it important that they should not be completely forgotten. Talked-down stories suggested that something called the Big Heat had also played a part. Dragons *loved* heat.

Even young dragons knew there had been something called *fighting* before the Great Ridding. That was long left behind, of course, because there were no enemies to fight any more. Although Dragons now prided themselves on being peace-loving, they knew that hadn't always been the case. They had once been fierce and powerful. Otherwise how could there have been the Great Ridding?

Oddly enough, they still liked to keep the names that suggested the Old Time and the old ways, which is how it came about that these proud dragon parents decided to call their son Ferocity. They thought it sounded very good with their family name, which was Bychaheadoff.

It wasn't until Ferocity was growing scales and fins on his back that his parents noticed his colour was – how best to put it? – *unusual*. They'd been wondering whether he was to be green, like Perilous, his mag; or black, like Rampant, his dag. But then the beige darkened and became...

"A sort of falling-leaf tint?" suggested his mag.

"Brown, then," said his dag. "Unexpected, but quite acceptable."

But then the brown seemed to drain away altogether, leaving only the red, which grew redder and redder until...

"It's obvious," whispered his mag, one dark after fire-out, peering down at her mumbo in a worried but loving way as he slept.

"No question at all," agreed his dag. "He isn't any of the usual dragon colours."

"What is he, then?" asked his mag, who thought she had the word for it on the tip of her tongue but didn't like to say it.

There was a stretch of silence between them.

"*I* know what he is," muttered a gruff voice behind them.

Rampant and Perilous whipped round to see a familiar shape emerge from the darkest part of their cave.

"Dag!" spluttered Rampant, pretending not to have got a terrible fright. "I didn't see you there."

Rampant's dag, a large, snaggle-toothed old dragon with a limp from an ancient flying injury, hobbled over to them. He peered down through heavy lids at his oddly hued grandmumbo.

"I'll tell you what he is. He's *red*."

"*Red?*" croaked Rampant. "But … that's *impossible*. There's never been a red dragon. Red dragons don't exist."

His old dag gave him a funny look and grunted, "Now one does. Yours."

Ferocity's parents talked

it over that dark, when Granddag had hobbled back into the shadows to a crevice in the rear of their cave, which he shared with his pair.

"Do you think there's anything actually *wrong* with being red?" asked Perilous hesitantly.

"Why would there be?" replied Rampant. "Red makes him ... er..."

"Different?" put in Perilous.

"Well, yes. But *every* dragon's different in his or her way. Being red – that makes him more ... more..."

"Interesting."

"Right! That's exactly what it makes him."

"And *special*," added Perilous, peering down at Ferocity, who looked adorable with his tail-point in his mouth.

"Oh, yes. Very, very special. If our mumbo's red, my dear, then red's what he's supposed to be."

There was a moment of silence.

"Perhaps there are others," said Perilous suddenly. "Red dragons, I mean – somewhere out there in the world."

"Yes, I expect so – lots of them," agreed Rampant. "But we never go anywhere so I guess we'll never know."

Perilous dropped her head and rested it on her pair's haunch. He covered her tenderly with his wing.

"You're so wise, my mild, decent love," she growled softly. Growls were fierce once – used to frighten uprights, mostly – but now they were only affectionate.

"Ferocity's a wonderful, strapping mumbo," said Rampant, "and for my part I'm proud he's different."

They crouched there quietly. Perilous felt a wave of contentment wash over her until, out of the corner of her eye, she noticed a trace of brown smoke drifting from Rampant's nostrils. Her head jerked up with sudden concern.

"What's the matter?"

"What? Nothing – why d'you ask?" He hastily sniffed the smoke back up his nose.

"You never blow smoke like that. Not unless something's wrong."

Rampant's think-space was filling with not-true-thinks, but his pair knew him too well, and deep down he was bursting to tell her anyway.

"Our coal supplies are running low," he said in a sort of spluttering cough. "I found out. It's all the Council can talk about."

In a corner of cave, Ferocity's eyes snapped open. He didn't understand much language yet but there was an unfamiliar tone to his dag's voice. A tone he didn't like. Could it be – what was the word – *fear*?

~◦✦◦~

By the time Ferocity was due to start dragon school, his parents had very nearly forgotten he was different. So it's easy to imagine their surprise when, on the light before he was due to start school, Head-dragon Heinous called them in for a quick heads-together in the big, shabby, crumbling-at-the-corners school built-thing, with the big hole in its flat top where a very tall dragon teacher had, in a moment of untypical annoyance, thrust his horns. Of course, when such not-decents damaged an old built-thing, there was no way to repair it, and most such shelters eventually crumbled away.

"It has come to my attention," Heinous began, "that your son is – how can I put it? – *red*."

"*Is* he?" replied Rampant, as if he'd never really noticed. "Well, now that you mention it, he is rather a fine shade of red, don't you think?"

"He has a wonderful think-space!" added Ferocity's mag.

Head-dragon Heinous looked at her sternly. "He would have, wouldn't he? All mumbos are bright."

"I think what my pair is trying to say," put in Rampant quickly, "is that we're sure Ferocity will be a credit to the school."

"Let's hope so, shall we?" replied Heinous. "But I was wondering whether … I mean, we prefer all our mumbo pupils to look … well, like … like *regular* mumbos, if you take my smoke-drift?"

The Bychaheadoffs shared a bemused look.

"Regular?" echoed Perilous.

"Yes. Very regular." Heinous lowered his voice slightly and leaned forward. "Your son will, I fear, stand out in the playground. If he were perhaps a rugged black like you, Rampant, or … or a delightful green like you, Perilous… What I'm trying to say is—"

"Yes, what exactly *are* you trying to say?" asked Rampant evenly.

Heinous took a deep breath. "Couldn't you arrange for him to *perhaps* roll in some mud—"

"*Mud?*" repeated Perilous sharply.

"Certainly – or take a dip in a pond of green slime—"

"*Slime?*" spluttered Rampant.

"Yes, or ... or..." Heinous spotted the dark trickle of smoke now seeping from the Bychaheadoffs' nostrils and added, "Nothing that would harm him, of course!"

Ferocity's parents rose to their full height.

"We are *not*," said Rampant, "going to roll our son in mud or dip him in any dirty stinking pond slime."

"Or anything else for that matter!" snorted Perilous.

"There is *nothing* wrong with his colour," Rampant continued. "As a matter of fact, we're very fond of it. Red is ... is... What is it, Perilous?"

"Different," answered his pair.

"In a good way," said Rampant firmly. "Now, Head-dragon, if you have a problem with it, we'll simply home-cave Ferocity instead." He coughed. "Good dragon-light to you."

When Ferocity's mag dropped him off on the first light of school, the other mumbos tried not to stare at him, which would have been undragonly rude. Rudeness was the opposite of politeness, and politeness was one of the first Rules of Dragonkind.

"*Put the kind into dragonkind!*" was something mumbos recited every single day at school. They meant it, too.

By the end of the second lesson, everyone had almost forgotten Ferocity's unusual colour. Teasing just wasn't done. One she-mumbo, Merciless, sidled up to him between lessons and asked politely *why* he was red.

"Why? How should I know? I was hatched like it."

"It's nice," Merciless said. "Can I nuzzle you now?"

There was something about the way she asked the question that sent a slightly uncomfortable tingle down Ferocity's back-fins.

"If you want," he replied a little anxiously.

And she did. Behind his ear. Which was surprisingly nice – and a bit tickly. Then she said, "Can I call you Red?"

Ferocity looked at her. He realized he quite liked the idea of a nickname.

"If you want."

And just like Ferocity when he spread his wings, the name took off in no time. It wasn't long before the whole class was calling him Red. And that was the name the other mumbos called him from that light onward.

CHAPTER 2

Red did well at school, just as his parents had expected – just as everyone had expected, because, as the head-dragon had said, "All mumbos are bright." And indeed, it was a well-known fact: all dragons were now clever. Red stood out only by seeming to be a bit *too* clever.

But that didn't stand in the way of him making friends. He may have been different, but the other mumbos liked him even more for his very special think-space than for his very special colour. It was what went on in there that made him say all sorts of things that set him apart. Like when he suggested, "Let's play Dragons and Uprights."

Dragons and *Uprights*? The other mumbos fell into stunned silence.

"What's wrong with that?" asked Red.

Basher, a bright green mumbo with a particularly

large head and noticeably sharp teeth, turned to him. "Uprights," he said, snarling, "are our worst enemies, driven out a long, long time ago when the fighting ended. We don't play games about *them*!"

"And anyway," added Fiery, a small black she-mumbo with knobbly horns, "they're gone from the mainland, which means the whole world." She gave a hoity grunt and added, "Don't you know *anything*?"

"Yeah!" scoffed Basher. "So why bother even thinking about stupid uprights?"

"I think about a lot of things," mumbled Red.

Thinks? They weren't that useful, his teacher would say. "Because the more thinks you have, the more confused you get. *Think* less. *Do* more."

The lessons the mumbos learned were limited to the things dragons needed to know. Or, more specifically, the things their teachers *thought* they needed to know. Which wasn't that much. Flying skills, for example, were important – like how to glide or soar or do a tail-over-horns, crash-land and, in the advanced classes, do straight-up take-offs. All very challenging when you're as bottom-heavy as dragons.

"If we were like sky-flappers," said Red to his

granddag one dark over supper, "it would be much easier to fly."

"If we were anything like sky-flappers," replied his granddag, sucking on a juicy ground-flapper bone by the fire, "we'd be the ones being eaten."

Granddag always said funny things like that.

Mumbos also learned Cave Law and Rules of Dragonkind, like talking-not-quarrelling, resisting strong *feelings* – ugh! – and displaying excellent dragon manners in school. Everything to do with how dragons should treat each other came together under one subject heading. "Say it again – louder this time," Berserk, a she-dragon-teacher, would roar.

"DECENCY!" the class would roar back. They enjoyed roaring, mostly because they weren't allowed to do it very much.

By the time Red and his classmates were fully scaled and their back-fins about half grown, their class teacher, Berserk, announced it was time to talk about the Facts of Smoke.

"At present, you blow white smoke when you're happy—"

Basher, always the first to demonstrate, blew a big puff of white smoke.

"Very good, Basher. Anyway, as you may unfortunately have realized, there'll be times in your full-grown lives when you'll *feel* things. Feelings are things we dragons don't really have good words for."

An excited murmur rose in the class. Fiery was first to raise her tail-point.

"Like what sort of things?" she asked, knowing several of them but enjoying watching her rather uptight teacher attempt to explain.

Berserk cleared her throat. "Things like anger, hate and … um … *envy*." The young teacher could hardly bring herself to say the last one. A shocked silence fell over the class. "These words," Berserk continued, her voice now lowered to a whisper, "are called swearing and are strictly forbidden."

Everyone knew about *swearing*. A mumbo could be kept in school for a whole free light if he or she said a swear word out loud. It was Red who raised his tail-point next.

"Yes, Red?"

"I just had a think—"

"Uh-oh," grunted Basher.

"If we *feel* things, we should definitely have good words for them because, well, feelings are very important things for a dragon to have."

The rest of the class turned and stared at Red. If dragons could have fallen about in fits of giggles they would have done.

The teacher cleared her throat again. "I'm not sure, Red, that I follow you," she said, even though, deep down, she probably did.

Red opened his mouth to answer but was suddenly aware of all the other mumbos staring at him.

"Nothing," he said awkwardly.

The teacher gave a little sigh of relief. "We don't have proper words for many of these ugly, indecent feelings," she said, "because we hardly ever have them. And when we *do* have them, something bad happens."

"Like what?" asked Basher, forgetting to raise his tail-point.

"Our smoke, our beautiful white dragon smoke, turns black. And," the teacher continued solemnly, "we try never to blow any of—"

Red interrupted. "My granddag said it was black smoke that covered the blue-top and ruined the whole world. He said uprights made black smoke and black smoke brought life-over."

"How does your granddag know that?" asked Basher.

"*Every* dragon should know it," explained Berserk. "Dragon smoke – the *white* kind – is for showing how different we are from those terrible *creatures* we banished in" – her eyes darted from one mumbo to the next – "in what?"

"THE GREAT RIDDING!" the whole class shouted.

"Correct. Our smoke is harmless – unless it's black. We must try never to blow that kind in case the badness in it gets out – the same way it did in the Old Time when uprights ruined the world with it—"

Red interrupted again. "My granddag said that ages ago, when the world was going bad, dragons gave uprights a chance to make griffilin—"

"Oooh! Red said the impossible word!" cried Merciless.

The other mumbos just looked puzzled.

"What's *griffilin*?" one of them asked.

"Don't waste your think-spaces on it. It can't happen. That's why we don't say it," warned Berserk.

"Why can't it?" asked Red.

The teacher gave him a stern look. "Because it would need uprights to listen. And listening's not what uprights do."

Fire was a topic that often came up in lessons, and was very important to dragons.

"Eat up your twigs and branches before meals," their teacher often stressed. "Without them, you won't have fire in your chests. And without *that*, well,

I won't even go into that because it's much too..." She cleared her throat. "Anyway, very soon you'll be able to chew and swallow coal."

The whole class shivered with excited anticipation.

"This will put fire in your chests," the teacher went on, "and one light you'll feel the urge all dragons feel, and you'll open your jaws and a stream of beautiful fire will flow from you. Then, and only then, will you stop being mumbos and become—"

"Full-grown dragons!" shouted Basher, thumping on the floor with his strong hind paws. "FULL-GROWN! FULL-GROWN! FULL-GROWN!"

The other mumbos, stirred by their classmate's words, joined in, chanting and thumping on the floor until the sound rang through the built-thing like thunder.

Later that light, Red – ever curious – caught up with his teacher in the school playground and asked, "Where does the coal we eat come from?"

The teacher gave him a very curious look. "I thought your dag was head coaler. I'm surprised he hasn't told you that."

"Coal stacks?" Red guessed. Berserk nodded. "Does it grow there?"

There was an uncomfortable silence. The teacher shifted slightly on her haunches. "It's there because" – she gave a little cough – "because it's … er … always been there." She began to edge away, but Red followed.

"But if all full-growns eat it, won't it eventually get used up?"

A faint trickle of darkish smoke drifted from the teacher's nostrils. "You ask too many questions, Ferocity. Try not to. It's unhealthy."

Red felt a stab of shame. "Sorry, I was just trying—"

"*Try* less. *Listen* more. Now repeat after me," said his teacher, staring at him earnestly. "*We eat coal to fuel our fires. Coal makes us whole and much better flyers.*"

Red repeated her words. But his think-space was alight with even more nagging, unanswered questions.

The mumbos only took one term of Geography (mostly because they never went very far), and it was mainly about the Endless Water. They were warned *never* to fly over it – even though they'd probably never see it – because dragons can't swim. Known fact.

The Geography teacher, Gruesome, made them recite a reminder:

"*Over the valleys and hills you can fly, but not over water; that way—*"

"*LIFE-OVER!*" the class all shouted.

Once every few lights, they practised blowing smoke signals, which is how dragons communicate across distances, even short ones. And they learned tail-signalling, a skill left over from Before Speak. Tail-signalling was a sort of forgotten language and most of the mumbos found it pointless – this was a joke because of their *tail-points*. But Red liked it. His dag had forgotten it completely from his school-lights, so Red and his friends could use it to talk in secret.

"You lot are really getting on my tail-point!" Rampant would complain whenever Red had his friends round to cave and they sent messages to one another in this way. "I can't understand a smoking word you're signalling. And that's rude."

No one liked being called rude, so they quickly stopped. Until the next time. One dark, Red saw his dag blow a trace of black – no, no, not black but *greyish* – smoke. He'd never once seen him do that, not even the time he went hunting horn-trotters and bashed his head on a branch mid-chase. So that was the end of tail-signalling, at least in cave. One thing was certain: no one wanted to see what happened when Rampant's grey smoke turned black.

Red's favourite subject was Dragonstory, also called the Trail of Smoke. It was passed down from full-growns to mumbos and went right back to when dragons weren't at all as they are today.

"There have been so many advances in dragonkind within the think-hold of our oldest dragons that it's no wonder we have changed and become far better in every way," another of his teachers, Bellicose, explained.

And like all good pupils, Red and the rest of his class believed everything they were told.

CHAPTER 3

Red loved school, but he always seemed to have more questions than his friends. When he sensed he wasn't going to get all the answers from his teachers, he would save them for when his mag and dag next went out, and his granddag and grandmag stayed in to mumbo-sit. They loved telling him about Dragonstory.

"For most of the Trail of Smoke," his grandmag said one dark, "we had mortal enemies."

"What does *mortal* mean?" asked Red, crunching a fur-hopper bone.

There was a slight pause.

"Well, go on," urged his granddag. "Tell him."

"It means deadly and cruel—"

"And violent!" added his granddag, and, despite himself, uttered a little growl.

"Granddag!" protested Red, shocked. "You said the *vi* word!"

His granddag muttered something.

"Pardon?" said Red.

His granddag, ignoring the pain in his old wobbly haunches, rose to his full height, spilling shadows against the cave walls that made him look twice the size. Now his words were very loud and very clear.

"I said: VIOLENT!" He cleared his throat and lowered his voice. "These words you hear at school – the ones they *say* are indecent – describe what dragons once *were* and could still *be*."

"*Still?*" Red just about managed to say it.

"YES! STILL!" His granddag gave a little rasping cough. "*Deadly* and *cruel* and *violent* should never have been left behind. They're words that we should always keep in our think-spaces."

"But why, Granddag? We don't need any of those awful things now!"

"In case," the old dragon hissed.

"In case what?"

"They ever come back."

Red shivered down his back-fins, he didn't know why.

Granddag bent his neck so that his snout was very close to Red's; close enough so the mumbo got a whiff of his granddag's acrid smoke-breath.

"If it's *cruel* to protect your family," the old dragon continued, "if it's *violent* to stand up for your kind; if *goodness* and *decency* come under threat; if every bit of your body goes tight with the agony of watching your own beautiful world disappear, then tell me – is it not right to use the old ways?"

Red opened his mouth to answer. But couldn't. There was another long silence, eventually broken by his grandmag suddenly nudging her pair and saying in a croaky voice, "Enough! That's enough now!"

One thing was clear to Red, and that was that the mere mention of that Old Time made his grandparents – all full-growns, in fact – very uncomfortable. This period of Dragonstory was very unpleasant and only taught to half-growns who were so nearly full-grown that they could breathe fire. But thanks to his granddag, Red found out about uprights earlier than most. "Those REPULSIVE clawless, fireless, wingless creatures!" he called them, who, despite being scaleless and puny, had once ruled the world, as dragons did today.

They were all gone now, most dragons believed. Thanks to the Great Ridding.

Neither Red's grandparents nor his parents – indeed, not even any teacher – could explain exactly how this had happened, because dragons now prided themselves on being civilized, and the thought of uprights and the Old Time stirred something so black in their think-spaces that they felt strange, forbidden thinks stirring inside them, making them hot behind their eyes, and sending shivers through their limbs right down to the tips of their very sharp claws.

Which is why it came as a shock when Red's granddag showed him his teeth one dark by the light of the fire.

"Here," the old dragon grunted, "take a good look at these. See how sharp they are?"

Red peered at them. Sure, they were a little worn down, but the mumbo still marvelled at their immense size and sharpness.

"You don't think dragons need these crunchers *just* for eating – even the few who are still meat-feeders?"

"Are they for crunching pieces of coal?" Red asked innocently.

The old dragon growled and shook his head. "Course not. We used them to drive out those stinking uprights."

"Drive them out, Granddag?"

There was a pause.

"Yes, son, yes. WE RIP-BURN-KILLED 'EM!"

There was an unfamiliar sound in the old dragon's voice – could it be *pleasure*?

Red gasped. *Rip-burn-kill* was the worst – the very worst – swearing he'd ever heard. And it left him talkless.

His granddag sensed the mumbo's shock. "We had to get rid of them somehow," he insisted. "Or what? As sure as fire burns bright, they'd have got rid of us. They nearly did!"

Red cleared his throat. There was something hot and bad and bitter-tasting in there, like rotten meat.

Still, he mustered a question. "What about the ones we didn't" – Red gulped – "do *that* to?"

"The unlucky ones who survived, you mean?" His granddag gave a chortling snort. "They fled as fast as their puny little legs could carry them."

"You sound like you've seen one, Granddag!"

"Who, me? Don't be ridiculous!" the old dragon snarled. "This was all long, *long* before my time! Just as well, because I'm certain eating one would've made all my teeth fall out!"

Nothing he'd heard so far shocked Red quite like this.

"EAT them? You mean dragons *ate* uprights?"

His granddag gave a grunt. "Well, it's all just stories – ages old. Who can really know for sure? No one, that's who…" With that he turned and hobbled off. "All I know is I'm no green-feeder, not me," he muttered as he vanished into the shadows, "but I don't suppose I could've stomached eating the likes of *them*."

Red called after him. "Where did they go, Granddag? The uprights, I mean. The ones who got away?"

His granddag's gnarled old face reappeared suddenly, eyes gleaming in the firelight.

"Go?" A faint trail of black smoke spurted from his nostrils. Then he said quite simply, "Wherever they went, they'd better FLAMING WELL STAY THERE!"

A little later, when Red asked his grandmag the same question, she fluttered her old wrinkled wings, ducked her head, and insisted there never really *were* any uprights. But Red knew that couldn't be right – it *couldn't* be – because dragons can't make things up. Their think-spaces just aren't made that way.

Later, when his dag came back to cave and stuck his head in to say good dragon-dark, Red put the same question to him. After huffing a little – to hold his smoke back, Red presumed – Rampant told him of the rumours that the upright survivors of the terrible pre-Ridding battles, if indeed there *were* any, were thought to be scattered on small live-places called *land-lumps* somewhere out in the Endless Water.

"That's a very, very long way away, where they can't harm anyone or anything," he assured his mumbo.

"How'd they get there, Dag?" asked Red sleepily.

"You mean *if* they got there."

"Yes."

"Nobody knows." Rampant leaned down and nuzzled his son's ear. "Now go to sleep, and don't waste your think-space on uprights. They're nothing but dust and shadows."

Reassured, Red gave a contented sigh, closed his eyes, and slipped away, deep into the vastness of his think-space.

Next time the subject of uprights came up at school, Red's class teacher backed up Rampant's words. She had no reason not to.

"We don't have to worry about marauding uprights any more, forever hunting us and taking over our live-spaces and then ruining them. If uprights did *anything* good, it was to show us, by their awful example, how *not* to live." Berserk looked severely at the class. "We dragons are very practical and concentrate on our needs and on just being polite and sensible. In a word...?"

"DECENT!" the mumbos replied. And then, as if on cue, they recited, *"We never quarrel or argue, it's true – kindness and decency's what dragons do."*

The teacher nodded. "When disagreements or problems arise, what do we do?" She scanned the mumbos hopefully until one, at the back of the class, raised her tail-point.

"Yes, Militant?"

"We solve them by talking-not-quarrelling."

"Talking-not-quarrelling. That's right. We crouch around a fire, and we have a – anyone…?"

This time the class answered in chorus, tail-signalling for emphasis: "HEADS-TOGETHER!"

"That's correct. We have a heads-together till we agree on what to do next. Who knows what we call that?"

"DRAGONSENSE!"

"It's polite to raise your tail-point *before* you answer, Ferocity. But yes. We never really need to quarrel. There's plenty of live-space, lots of fruit and other green-feed, and small prey for the few of us who, regrettably" – her eyes darted to Basher – "are still meat-feeders. So we're not short of food."

Red's tail-point shot up. "So what *are* we short of?"

"Why d'you ask that, Ferocity?"

"Well, the way you said *food* sounded as if we were short of *something*."

Their teacher gave an irritable little cough. "Let's move on, please…"

Talk of food reminded Red of a subject that sometimes caused not quarrels but discussions in cave. His dag had recently given up meat-feeding, calling it *uncivilized* because it involved life-ending.

"Nasty business," Rampant had said. "I like to think of dragonkind as having moved beyond that. I hope when you're older, son, you'll follow my example." He'd thrown a meaningful glance at his pair. She, on the other paw, was an extremely skilled hunter who refused to deny her son the "fire-stoking pleasures" of a meat diet.

"You want to be a green-feeder, go right ahead, dear," she'd said. "Me? I *end* what I eat."

Ferocity hadn't known which parent to side with. What he did know was that he absolutely loved the taste of ground-flapper.

Suddenly his teacher's voice snapped him out of his back-thinks.

"Another example of talking-not-quarrelling," she said solemnly, "is deciding how to share out the coal for our chest-fires – yes, all right, Merciless, no need to show us your smoke rings."

Red needed to listen very carefully to coal-talk. His dag, as head coaler, crouched on the Council and had to attend heads-togethers. Red had overheard his parents talking about this recently after fire-out. He wondered with a sharp realization if coal was the answer the teacher had avoided giving before – could *that* be what they were short of?

"One last thing," the teacher added. "Listen very carefully, because this may very well be the difference between life and life-over for us dragons." The class fell silent. "You must – *must* – keep your chest-fires lit at all times. No exceptions. Does anyone here know why?"

Silence.

"Because if your chest-fire goes out, you stop being" – she lowered her voice to a whisper – "a *full-dragon*."

There was a gasp, followed by excited murmurs. Berserk raised her tail-point for silence.

"Not being a full-dragon means you can't breathe fire, and if you can't do that, you can't fly!"

Another uneasy murmur from the class.

"We have a signal for that, mumbos." And she showed them by curving her tail to point to her chest.

She cleared her throat uneasily. "*That* is the most terrible signal you can *ever* make. I only hope that none of you ever have to." Then she uncurved her tail and said pleasantly, "Good dragon-light, everyone."

CHAPTER 4

For more lights and darks than he could remember, Red had been waiting for one thing, and he wasn't alone. From a very young age, every mumbo learned that the Special Place was by far the most important thing in the whole of their live-space. Roughneck, teacher of Dragonstory, had waited patiently for the moment when the Council would give their permission for the school to visit it.

That light had finally come.

The Special Place was a built-thing on the edge of Red's live-space that had somehow not fallen down. He and his mag sometimes passed it when they went to visit his dag at work, but then the doors were always hard shut.

They weren't shut now.

This light, the doors were open wide and there were special guides to show them where to go. The mumbos

broke into pairs to squeeze through the entrance –
a straight-sided opening quite unlike a cave mouth.

This built-thing was the strangest, most solemn Red
had ever been in.

He stood with the rest of his class, shuffling a little
but otherwise still and silent, staring all around him.
From the ground to the roof, stretching from side to
side, were flat bits of wood, and arranged along these
were a lot of similar objects, large and small, thick
and thin. The inside was hollow and straight shaped,
and everything in it was grey with dust and sticky-
spinners' homes.

Red's dag always said uprights had lived not sensibly
in caves but un-sensibly in built-things. No one knew
why. *Caves* were what you lived in. Most upright things
dragons saw no use for. Those were just scattered about,
or in the way, and probably dangerous considering the
state that the world had been left in. So, many warms
and colds ago, dragons had dug huge pits – their big,
heavy, well-clawed forepaws were perfectly adapted for
digging – pushed in as much of this useless rubble and
trappings as they could, and buried them. Since then,
nature had reclaimed these ugly areas, which became
play-lands or hunt-lands for dragonkind.

But the Special Place was one upright thing they didn't bury.

Roughkneck lifted one of these objects off its wood-strip with his teeth and laid it carefully on the ground for all to see.

"This, mumbos, is a Block of Knowledge. We know very little about it. Except" – his eyes fell on the class – "that it was *caused* by uprights."

The class came alive with whispers, and a few gasps.

"Of course, we don't have any idea what uprights *looked* like. What we do know is that they caused things, some of which are still part of dragons' lives. Built-things, like the one we're standing in, and, of course, our own beloved school."

There had been occasions when Red had looked at his school and thought how often full-growns talked about how stupid uprights had been compared with dragons. But there was something that always puzzled him: no dragon he knew could have *caused* the built-things that uprights had left. Now he thought the same think about this one.

The teacher continued. "Those horrific creatures, *before* they ruined everything and before they were banished, caused all sorts of things – but these things right here, our wisest dragons believe, may well be the most important of all." He paused. "Right. You may sniff it, but absolutely NO touching or licking."

The class jumped closer and took turns sniffing.

"Phew!" spluttered Basher, reeling back. "Doesn't smell like anything I've ever smelled before!"

"Ugh! Disgusting!" snorted Fiery.

Red took a sniff. "Lovely," he said with quiet reverence.

The others eyed him strangely.

"You say the weirdest things," whispered Militant.

"Don't judge a block by its smell, mumbos," said the teacher, and raised his tail-point for silence. "Now. Have any of you ever wondered why it is that for so many warms and colds, we ran away from uprights, even though they were puny, pathetic, little—" He stopped himself abruptly, and gave a sharp cough. "So much smaller and weaker than us?"

The mumbos fell silent.

"It was because they had the Power of the Hand."

The mumbos exchanged bemused glances. Only Red had the nerve to ask, "What is the *haaaand*?"

The teacher gave a little grunt. "If you want to know *that* you'd better ask an upright. And since there aren't any left, we'll just have to hope that one of our wiser dragons will eventually find the answer. Any more questions? Right, everybody out."

The mumbos turned and filed solemnly out of the hollow space. Every one of them felt something very special had just happened, but none of them knew quite what.

Back at cave that dark, Red was struggling to sleep. After the excitement of the visit, all he had seen in the Special Place filled his think-space. Especially the mysterious Blocks of Knowledge. What could they be? They had smelled almost good enough to eat.

Now he could hear voices. Not in his head, but close by.

He opened his eyes and saw his mag and dag huddled once again by the embers of the fire in a heads-together. They were talking in agitated whispers. He could hardly hear anything, but he caught the familiar word *coal*. And an unfamiliar one: *mission*.

BLOCK II
THE
MISSION

CHAPTER 5

At first lesson the next light, Red was called to the front of the class to talk about anything that interested him. Of course, there was only one thing on his think-space: the mission. His dag had made it clear he shouldn't talk about "Council things". But he couldn't hold it in.

He stood for a long moment staring anxiously out. He could see Berserk, his teacher, looking at him impatiently. He suddenly blurted out, "My family are leaving cave!"

There was uproar. Even Berserk looked concerned. She shuffled nervously.

"I beg your pardon?" she said. "What exactly do you mean – *leaving* cave?"

Basher, bashing the floor with one foot, shouted, "No one's ever left cave, Red!"

Fiery shook her head, huffed and recited, *"We don't get detached. We stay where we're hatched!"*

Even Militant, usually a calm little mumbo, jumped up and said, "Your family must have lost their flaming think-spaces!"

It wasn't long before the whole class had left their crouch-places to crowd round Red with anxious puffs of smoke. Finally Berserk raised her tail-point for silence.

"All right, all right," she said firmly. "Everyone, calm down; that's enough fuss... Let's hear what Ferocity has to say. CROUCH DOWN!"

The mumbos returned reluctantly to their places.

"Well, the thing is ... er ... the thing is..."

"Yes? What *is* the thing, Ferocity?" asked Berserk curiously.

"The thing is, we – I mean, my family and me—"

"My family and *I*," his teacher corrected.

"My family and *I* are going on a mission."

"What's a *mission*?" a voice from the back of the class asked.

Red didn't answer. How could he? He didn't have the faintest think what a mission actually was. He'd just heard his dag say they were going on one. And now he heard himself repeating the word vaguely. "*Mission...*"

The word was so unusual, not even his teacher appeared to know what it meant. More reason for Red to be proud that his dag knew it. Rampant learned a lot of funny words from his job with the Council. Suddenly a think came to Red. Dragons may all be clever now. But some, like my dag, must be cleverer than others.

Red cleared his throat. "The Council knows."

"Did I hear you say the *Council*?" interrupted Berserk.

"Yes. They told my dag about the mission. And that it was secret."

There was a hush.

"Secret?" echoed his teacher in an accusatory way. "But everyone knows that dragons don't do secrets."

The class erupted into agitated tail-signalling and smoke-blowing and foot-thumping until Berserk stopped them.

"A mission may not be usual," she said, "but if the Council says it's important – secret or otherwise – then THAT is what it must surely be."

Tails dropped, loud voices faded to whispers, and the class shuffled off to their next lesson.

One thing was certain. If there'd been any doubt in any of his classmates' think-spaces that Red was a bit different before, there wasn't any now. It didn't help when Berserk, who'd tried hard not to show her true feelings in class, was heard afterwards, mumbling under her smoke-breath, "Dragons leaving cave on a *mission* – and a *secret* one at that! Outrageous!"

Of course, no one had anything against Red himself. But it was … *different*. And different made your fins stand on end.

~✣~

When Red got home from school, he asked his mag, "Why do we have to leave cave? Dragons don't do that, do they?"

His mag didn't say anything for a while. She just laid some sky-flappers on the floor in front of him. The smell was comforting, especially on a light as embarrassing and awkward as this one had been. He snatched one and swallowed it down in a single gulp.

Dragons have a sort of halfway-down extra stomach, where food gets cooked as it passes their chest-fires. Red let out a burned-sky-flapper-smelling BUURRP! that echoed round the cave. Suddenly he felt bad about not being able to resist meat, and admired his dag for being beyond it.

As for the coal, until recently he'd just eaten charred wood fragments. Coal wasn't as tasty as proper food, and much harder to crunch up and swallow. His mag pointed sternly with her tail at their coal pile, and Red gave a gusty sigh.

"Don't waste it on me," he mumbled. "I've tried and tried. I'll never be able to breathe fire, so what's the tail-point—"

"NEVER?" His dag's booming voice made Red turn just in time to see his bulk appear in the mouth of cave clutching a couple of bushes in his claws. "You want to be a full-dragon? Or are you going to stay a smoke-blowing wuss the rest of your life?"

"Rampant, please!" hissed Perilous. "Ferocity's just not quite ready yet." And she gave her mumbo a reassuring little nuzzle.

Rampant jumped into cave and threw the bushes on the floor. He stared at his son. "Tell me something. Can the others in your class breathe fire yet?"

"I don't know," Red said uncomfortably. "Maybe."

"Don't worry your think-space about it," his mag soothed. "When it happens, it happens. You blow smoke as long as you like, dear."

"Nonsense! A mumbo must learn," snorted Rampant, and he came and stood over Red, looking stern, the reflection of flames from the fire dancing over his long snout and pricked ears, and flashing off his shoulder scales.

"Now," he ordered. "Show me your smoke."

"Pardon?"

"Show me your smoke, son!"

Ferocity looked up. Breathing fire was a critical stage in growing up, every mumbo knew that. Not having reached it yet was already weighing heavily on him. But disappointing his dag? That weighed heavier.

Red took a deep breath and felt his chest-fire glow.

"That's right, son. Can you feel it deep in your chest?" Red nodded. "Good. Now blow it out."

Red obeyed, but all that emerged from his jaws was plain, flameless white smoke.

"Bah!" sneered Rampant.

"Yes," put in Perilous. "That's what we *want* our son to blow: nice, polite smoke—"

"Polite! Polite will only get you so far!" Granddag's voice came growling from the fireside.

"Stop it, Granddag," said Perilous. "You'll confuse the poor mumbo."

"Dag's right," said Rampant. "You never know. There may come a time – and soon – when he has to stop being polite and start being—"

"SCARY!" growled Red's granddag.

"All right, Dag, calm down. I think we get the smoke-drift!" said Rampant.

"But I – I don't *want* to be scary," mumbled Red.

Rampant turned and looked down at his son. The sweet mumbo gazing up at him sent tiny tremors through the full-grown's whole body, but he resisted the temptation to nuzzle him. This wasn't a nuzzling occasion.

"Son. We'll start by learning to blow the right smoke. Save the flames for later."

"What's this all about, Rampant?" asked Perilous, clacking her wings nervously.

"WE'VE GOT A MISSION!" he roared.

His pair shot him a look. Her tone changed. It became a sort of low, warning growl.

"Lower your roar, dear," she said, eyes staring right at him. "As the saying goes: *Roar no more. Roars mean—*"

"*WARS!*" growled Granddag.

"I knew that!" Rampant muttered. Then he took a deep breath and said to Perilous, "On this mission of ours we may need all of our chest-fires to do some real Old Time dragon work."

"Old Time work?" said Perilous. "What does *that* mean?"

"It means" – Rampant lowered his voice – "that if we don't find a way to get more coal soon, being *polite* will be the least of our worries."

That dark, when Granddag and Grandmag were snoring loudly by the fire and Red and his mag were alone (Rampant had gone off to an emergency Council heads-together), Red asked her to tell him exactly what their mission was. She answered as best she could.

"Your dag hasn't told me much – Council rules. All I know is that it's to do with our coal supplies. We've almost used everything the uprights left behind. Your dag's job has always been to make sure the coal was shared out fairly, but there's more to it now – to do with Blocks of Knowledge. You know about those, right?"

Red thought of his recent visit to the Special Place. His feelings of puzzled awe were still fresh in his think-space.

"Mag," he asked, "do you know about *hands*?"

Perilous looked at him. What a wonderful, curious mumbo he was.

"No one really knows. Something – an upright part, perhaps – like a tail, or paw. Whatever they were, they must have been very clever and ... and..."

"What, Mag?"

It was that shiver down his back-fins again. Except worse this time. All Red could hear now was the faint crackle of the fire.

Then his mag whispered, "There's just no getting round it, son. Whatever they were, hands gave uprights their great advantage."

All dragons are raised to be very certain about things. And once again, Red wasn't.

"Mag," he said quietly, "are you *sure* dragons were cleverer than uprights?"

Perilous flinched. Her tone changed. She sounded more like herself.

"Ferocity! You know it's against the Rules of Dragonkind to ask questions like that. But, well, we believe that far back along the Trail of Smoke, the heat in the world made us bigger—"

Red broke in by reciting, *"Then came the Big Heat, that's all we know, when all that good hotness made think-spaces grow."*

"Yes. Our think-spaces got bigger too, while theirs – uprights', I mean – got smaller, and all their live-spaces started to rot." She nuzzled him gently. "A hotter world was very good for us and very bad for them. Next thing, they became fewer and fewer, and we became more and more. Still. They had the Power of the Hand, and used it to cause more hurt. In the end our back-parents couldn't stand it any more and decided to get rid of them once and for all."

"In the Great Ridding!"

"Yes."

This time they recited together: *"The Great Ridding came; we drove uprights away. Now we're alone, and alone we will stay!"*

Perilous drew herself up proudly and patted her

chest. "It's a dragons' world now, son, a dragons' world. And every day I thank Flame for it. Uprights didn't deserve a perfect world to live in, with all of their trappings and all of their wars."

At this, Granddag gave a sudden, unsettling grunt by the fire.

Red sat up. "What's *wars*, Granddag?" he asked.

His mag let out a plume of dark smoke. "You're still too young to know about—"

"WARS!" growled the old dragon, despite the warning. "Wars are one of the worst things uprights ever caused. Even when they weren't fighting us, they were rip-burn-killing *each other*."

"Granddag!" hissed Perilous.

"What? If a mumbo's old enough to see the Special Place, he's old enough to hear the truth."

Red jumped to his feet. "But, Granddag. Why did they do it – why did they cause wars, I mean?"

"Why?" The old dragon hobbled over and snatched a sky-flapper up in his jaws and gulped it down. "Who knows *why* uprights did any of the terrible things they did? All we know for certain is that they must have *liked* wars."

"Why?"

"Because they caused so many of them!"

For the rest of that dark, Red's think-space was bursting with questions about rip-burn-kills, unspeakable words, not-clever uprights and their very clever hands. He thought of the Special Place, crumbling now, but once – many warms and colds ago – perhaps something wonderful. And suddenly he understood: the word *built* must mean the same as *cause* – but more.

Maybe a lot more.

CHAPTER 6

It's not generally known, but dragons are distantly related to kangaroos. Not only are they shaped a bit like them, but both male and female dragons have pouches on their stomachs – very useful for carrying things in. So, when the Bychaheadoffs were preparing to set off on their mission, they were able to take a few things with them. Red soon found out that he was expected to fill his small pouch with pieces of coal.

"You're giving him *coal*, Rampant?" asked Perilous, suspiciously. "How far are we going?"

Rampant glanced at her. "As far as we have to."

His pair stuffed her pouch too, making it bulge and look very uncomfortable. Red reluctantly picked up some small lumps with his teeth and dropped them into his own pouch, holding it open with one side-claw. When Red asked his dag what *he* was taking, Red was astonished at what he showed him.

"You're taking a *Block of Knowledge*?"

Rampant's eyes darted this way and that, and he lowered his voice. "Not so loud. You want *everyone* to hear?"

"What are you taking a Block of Knowledge for, Dag?" whispered Red.

Rampant shrugged. "The Council told me to."

Red looked at it very carefully as his dag prepared to slip it into his pouch. It was large with strange marks on the front, and almost too heavy for his dag to lift with his front teeth.

"But why *that* one, Dag?"

Rampant snorted. "The Council just said it might help. They said it contained" – he coughed uncomfortably – "secrets."

Secrets? That word again.

The two old dragons shuffled out of the shadows at the back of the cave.

"You off, then?" grunted Granddag.

"When will you be back?" asked Grandmag, the knobbly tips of her wings quivering slightly.

"Soon as we can," said Rampant. "If you need anything, just ask the Council."

"The Council?" growled Granddag. "I don't need

any help from *them*. I don't need any help from anyone. Just…" He coughed slightly, as if choking down his feelings. "Come back."

"Dragons always come back, Dag."

"Perhaps that's because they never go anywhere," mumbled Grandmag, and hobbled back to the fireside.

Rampant led the way up to their usual take-off place at the top of a rocky hill. Below it, the countryside stretched away, caveless and dragonless as far as the eye could see. Rampant crouched and spread his wings. Red and his mag followed his example,

letting the wind caress the fine leathery undersides of theirs. Then Rampant roared, "Family – TAKE OFF!"

The three of them launched themselves upward. They flapped strongly to stay airborne – the first part was always the trickiest – and soon they were riding the warm air currents, leaving their live-place and all that was known and safe behind.

The dragon family flew as far as they could manage without a rest. By the time they landed again and prepared to spend the dark in the open, Red was more tired than he'd ever been – even on his longest practice flights at school.

Dragons are cold-blooded, which is why they love fires and light-shine. The family huddled coolly together under the sky-sparks and went to sleep.

Before they dropped off, Red asked his dag, "Are we nearly there yet?"

"No. We've only just got started."

Next light their first meal was whatever they could find – which was very little – and Red soon began to miss the simple pleasures of cave and their regular habits. He even missed school.

He helped his mag hunt – something he wasn't very good at. He was too slow and inexperienced to catch the fast ground-runners and, to be honest, he didn't much like ending them. But eating plants was nearly that worst of all feelings – *boring*. Red thought it rather odd that his dag could live on green stuff. When he asked his mag, she agreed.

"You know your dag. He's a dragon of principle," she said firmly, but Red got the feeling that she thought there was something distasteful – undragonlike, even – about the whole green-feed thing.

"You wouldn't catch *me* eating what fuzzy-bleaters eat," his granddag always said. "Our crunchers are meant for cutting not chewing."

As it was, Perilous made do with smaller prey, things she could easily snap up in one gulp without the nasty business that Rampant might find upsetting. The part of the meal Red enjoyed least was at the end when his mag drew a lump of coal out of her pouch with her front teeth and set it in front of him.

"Lump it and like it, as the saying goes," she said, and left him to it.

The full-growns limited themselves to a piece each, not much bigger than his.

"We're going to have problems keeping our chest-fires hot on this lot," remarked Perilous, taking her time and savouring every crunchy bite.

"The Council said we have to be sparing," said Rampant, and he blew out a white-hot flame to prove that the ration was enough. "We only have a few more lights and darks left before supplies run out," he said, spreading his wings. "And we might still have a long way to go."

"But how do you know the way, Dag?" Red asked as they flapped and flapped and slowly rose into the sky.

"I CAN SMELL IT!" Rampant roared back over his wing.

"What can you smell, Dag?" Red shouted.

"THE ENDLESS WATER!"

A rush of excitement hit the little red dragon and helped carry him higher.

He'd heard of the Endless Water, of course, but he'd never seen it. Once, when it had rained and rained and water had gathered in the pits in the earth near their live-place, his grandmag had pointed and said, "See those, Ferocity? If those were bigger – much, *much* bigger – and there was no end to them, they'd be like the Endless Water."

Red snapped out of the back-think and called, "Will the coal be there, Dag – near the Endless Water?"

"OR OVER IT!"

Perilous let out a barking shout of alarm. "Rampant! What are you roaring about? You can't mean we're going to fly *over* it?"

Red repeated the Endless Water recite between

wingbeats. *"Over hills and valleys, we're sure to ascend – but fly over water and that way we'll—"*

"Stop it, Ferocity!" shouted Rampant. "That's bring-down-talk, and that'll make your wings weak. They need to be strong! STRONG FOR THE MISSION!"

And with that, the huge black dragon banked steeply and flew on at a sharp angle. Red followed but he felt a shiver run through his whole body.

A shiver of fear.

BLOCK III
THE
TOWN-PLACE

CHAPTER 7

The dragon family flew, then rested, then flew some more. All the time, the strange salty smell in the air grew stronger, drawing Rampant on.

Next light, not long after setting off, Red glanced down and saw something unfamiliar in the landscape below – something *not* green and brown, as good dragon lands should be.

"What's that down there?" Red shouted over the sound of the wind against their wings.

"Nothing!" his dag shouted back.

"Can we go down and have a look?" called Red eagerly. He'd heard a few things about upright live-spaces. His teachers had called them *town-places* and warned them to stay as far from them as possible.

"What for?" asked his dag, glancing at the scene below, then snorting in disgust. "It's nothing but old upright rubbish."

"Please, Dag! Let's explore. Just for a little while! I need a rest, anyway."

"Go on," Perilous called out from behind. "We might as well, now that we're flying over it."

Rampant let out a reluctant growl, but he felt it too – a rather undragonlike gnawing curiosity. "We're not staying for long!" He circled downward, buffeted by updraughts that made steering tricky, his family following.

Once on the ground, Red settled his wings and looked around. In their live-spaces, most of what uprights had left had been cleared and buried many warms and colds ago. But here – where it seemed no dragons had ever been – their remains were everywhere.

"Why didn't dragons want to live here?" Red asked, sniffing a pile of rubble at his feet.

His dag looked around wearily. "Nothing here for dragons," he said.

"There might be trappings!" exclaimed Red. "I'd like to find some of those."

He'd heard that word – *trappings* – spoken around cave, and even once or twice in school, but he'd never actually *seen* any and had only a vague idea that they were clever things caused by the Power of the Hand.

Now might be his chance to understand their old enemy a bit better.

"Can we, Dag? Can we look for some?"

"Trappings are for uprights, not dragons," his dag said gruffly.

But moments later, and with an urging nudge from his mag, Rampant was leading the way across an open space towards a big built-thing. They found the entrance hole too small for a full-grown to squeeze through.

"Upright wrong, dragon strong!" Rampant muttered the old saying, and, as if to prove it, threw his powerful shoulder against the edge of the opening, which fell away, leaving room for them to squeeze in one at a time, very cautiously.

They'd all been in built-things before, but this one was different. For a start, it had a strange undragonlike smell.

"This place stinks," mumbled Rampant. "One thing's for sure: no dragon's ever set foot in here."

It was like their cave, dark and closed in, but the walls and the roof were flat.

"It's a bit like school, and the Special Place," said Red thoughtfully.

"I don't like it," hissed his mag.

"Told you," Rampant muttered. *"Upright places are all disgraces."*

"But we use them, don't we?" Red asked.

"We *tolerate* them. But never until they've had a good smoke-out to get rid of the stench!"

"Come on, Rampant," said Perilous. "You've never smelled an upright in your life."

"Don't need to," he huffed. "Some things you just know."

His pair inhaled deeply, nostrils flaring. "What you can smell," she said, "is rot and fur-crawlers. Which reminds me – I'm starving."

The dragons explored for a long time. Red's dag was very snout-in-the-air about the place, puffing out the odd cloud of dark smoke to express his disdain. But the trappings secretly fascinated him. They fascinated all of them, especially Red: a curved white thing, for instance, like an empty pool, covered in dust and tiny-crawlers, in one corner.

"Look! I could wash in that if it was outside and filled with rainwater."

"In that disgusting-looking thing?" snorted his mag. "What's wrong with a nice hot pool or a stream?"

"Your mag's right," grunted Rampant, staring down at it. "Why did uprights cause so many things when they had them everywhere already?"

There were other spaces too that had very complicated trappings made of wood. Red stared at the objects and couldn't help having thinks he knew were disloyal to his kind. Truth was, he just didn't see how you could start with a tree and finish with something like these things.

"Dag," he said. "Are you *sure* we were cleverer than uprights?"

Rampant stopped exploring with his tongue and turned round, eyes ablaze.

"OF COURSE I'M SURE!" he bellowed, so loudly that a black cloud of sky-flappers rose and flew away in fright from a nearby built-thing. "If uprights were the clever ones, then why are we here and *they're* long gone?"

The three dragons jumped along the wide, straight space that cut through all the rubble and abandoned trappings until they came to another big built-thing that was still more or less whole. They went inside. It was full of smaller open spaces. On the walls, or half hanging off them, were objects so strange and shocking that the dragons stood in front of them, frozen smokeless.

Red was first to speak, but only in a whisper.

"What are *those*?" he asked, peering at them in wonder.

His parents edged closer, their huge claws making scraping sounds on the hard floor. Rampant let his long forked tongue reach out until the tips touched one of the objects.

"Well?" his pair whispered.

The tongue snapped back as if the thing he was touching was so cold, it might freeze it.

"Uprights!"

"*What?*"

"Not *real* ones … look-likes."

Rampant's booming voice echoed around them, making old grey dust slip, like tiny waterfalls, from wooden strips on the walls. The other two gasped.

"How d'you *know*, Rampant?" asked Perilous.

"They stand upright. What else can it be? They

found a way to … to capture themselves, like looking down into a pool, and somehow holding it."

"But there's no water," pointed out Red.

"No," said his dag, peering at the object again, and giving it a little sniff.

"Clever…" murmured Red under his breath.

Rampant heard and shot him a look. "No, son. It's NOT clever. It's ugly and useless…"

Red's curiosity had already led him further along the wall, where he found more of the strange look-likes hanging. Others were lying on the floor, covered in dust. One of these showed something he recognized.

"Look. Here's things we eat … and alive things," he said. Some impulse made him put out his tongue – "Ugh! Doesn't taste, though!" – and he withdrew it again quickly.

"Ferocity, come away from that at once!" Perilous jumped over to him, gazing at the flat things on the wall. "They must have had live prey too, and green-feed. But instead of eating it all" – she peered closer – "they made these flat, tasteless things."

"But why?" wondered Red.

"Why? Always *why*. You have far too many whys for a mumbo."

"Grandmag says answers need questions."

"I haven't the first think what that means," snorted his dag.

But Red had already moved on to another object that showed an upright. He looked at it for some time, sniffing very cautiously but not daring to lick this time.

"Which are its hands?" Red asked.

His mag shuffled up beside him. "Those, maybe?" she guessed, pointing with her tail at some dangly bits at the end of its front legs.

"They don't *look* very powerful," muttered Rampant.

"Or very clever or dangerous," added Perilous.

"They look sad," observed Red.

His mag and dag glanced at him quizzically.

"Sad? What do you mean?" asked Perilous.

"I don't know exactly … just a feeling."

"Not *those* again," muttered his dag, scornfully.

In another open space near by, there were even stranger objects. Not flat like the look-likes, but rounded out, and standing on the floor. These must be uprights too, Red thought, and now he could see much more clearly what they'd looked like, though it was hard to judge their size.

"If they'd been as big as some of these," he said to his

mag and dag, "they might have been as powerful as a—"

"Don't say it!" Rampant growled. "Don't you *dare* say it."

The full-growns sniffed the objects suspiciously and explored with their tongues, while Red jumped, unnoticed for an instant, through an opening into another big not-cave. Moments later, he let out a noise that was as near to a roar as any half-grown can make.

"MAG! DAG! COME AND LOOK AT THIS!"

They came swiftly.

Red was standing, jaws agape, in front of an upright.

"This one's huge!" he said.

It was standing on a block of stone, and it was made of stone too. In what might have been its hand, it held something – a long stick sharpened at the end, like a dragon's tail-point. It was obviously just going to stick the point into something that lay below it, something that looked as real as any—

Rampant hissed, "It's trying to stick that point into one of US!"

Suddenly Red felt a warmth in his chest, and, without even meaning to, he breathed out a gout of black smoke. It felt hot on his tongue – but not

good-hot – and down his nose.
It mixed with the dark smoke
wafting over his shoulders from
the chest-fires of his mag and dag.

"See? What did I tell you?"
growled Rampant to his
pair. "Bringing our
son here was
a mistake –
a mistake!
Now look
at him: he's angry."

The black dragon jumped over to the red one and
began to nudge him firmly towards the hole in the wall
with his snout.

"That's ENOUGH! I've had all I can take of this
AWFUL place."

CHAPTER 8

The following light, as the family crested some particularly high hills, Red saw something strange up ahead. Where the sky met the land was a bright, shimmering line.

"Look, Dag! What's that?" he asked, squinting.

"I know what I think it may be – the Endless Water."

"The Endless Water?" hissed Perilous, horrified. "Are you sure?"

Rampant didn't answer at first. He just kept flying. "When we reach it," he shouted, "we'll rest. I don't know how far we'll have to fly before we see land again."

"See land *again*?" Red repeated. He exchanged an appalled look with his mag. "But, Dag!" he cried. "You can't mean we're going to fly *over* it?" Rampant didn't answer. "But you know the law!"

"There's only one law now – SURVIVAL."

With just a few powerful flaps, Perilous caught up with her pair.

"What are you saying, Rampant? Where are you taking us?"

Rampant gave her what he hoped was a casual side glance. "No need to worry."

"No need to—? Rampant, are you *listening* to me? WE ARE NOT FLYING OVER THE ENDLESS WATER!" Grey fear-smoke streamed from Perilous's nostrils. "When you told me about this mission, you never said anything about crossing—"

"Of course I did!"

"*Land,* Rampant!" He ignored her. "I SAID, LAND!" Perilous banked sharply and headed downward.

Rampant called after her. "Where in Flame are you going?"

But his pair wasn't listening. Not any more.

Red wondered if his mag had spotted some tasty morsel below – a sky-flapper, perhaps, or a land-hopper – and followed her excitedly. Moments later, his dag slowed and banked, his roar of frustration lost in the wind as he circled back round towards them.

"The truth is, you didn't say a thing about it – not a word."

They'd alighted on a high rocky perch buffeted by sharp gusts of wind, making it difficult for Red to keep his balance. There was a heads-together happening – sort of. Rampant was trying his best to calm his pair down.

"Now listen to me, will you—"

"I've finished listening, Rampant! Now you'd better listen to *me*. Dragon law clearly forbids it. And you know how I feel about" – her voice cracked suddenly – "*water.*"

"I know dragon law, and I know all about that old business with the big-wet—"

"Old business? *Old?* Rampant! I NEARLY DROWNED!"

"Bit of an exaggeration. It was an accident; your mag was old. She had no business flying. Anyway, I rescued you, didn't I?"

"Yes – *eventually* – but that was just a big-wet. This is the Endless Water. You think you could rescue me and Ferocity if we tired and came down somewhere out there?" She shook her head vigorously. "No … NO, Rampant! I would risk it for dragonkind, but there's NO WAY I'm taking our son—"

Red broke in. "It'll be all right, Mag; I'll make it. Don't worry about me. You know what a strong flyer I am."

"Yes, Ferocity, but you've never flown far. None of us have. And Endless means far – *very* far."

Rampant took a deep breath. His tone changed. "You're right. I should have told you, but I was afraid that if I did you wouldn't have agreed to come."

"You're flaming well right I wouldn't! And I wouldn't have let you bring our son!"

A strong gust of wind hit them suddenly, and they

all gripped hard with their back claws on the rocks and half opened their wings to steady themselves.

"Mag? Dag? Are you … *quarrelling*?" asked Red, shocked.

His parents answered together. "Dragons don't *do* quarrelling."

"What *are* you doing, then?"

"We're having a heads-together," said his mag.

"And coming to a decent agreement," added his dag. There was a pause, then Rampant went on. "Thing is, we've come all this way, and we really don't have any choice."

"What's *that* supposed to mean?" huffed Perilous.

"The Council chose me for this mission. And I made them a promise: to find coal, however far we have to travel, however long it takes. Everyone back home is depending on us." Another gust whipped across his snout. "I have a *duty* – a solemn dragon duty – and, as my family, so do you." He turned and looked at his son. "As for Ferocity, I told them I didn't want to bring him – the Council insisted!"

"Insisted? How dare they! He's just a mumbo – what difference can *he* make?"

There was a considered pause.

"I don't know. The Council said—"

"I don't want to hear any more about the flaming Council! He's not going one more flap!"

It was just too awful to sit there and listen to them; Red couldn't take it any longer. So he began to recite: *"Dragon families aren't like fur or feather: they don't drift apart; they stick together."* And he flapped his wings insistently. "We have to stick together, Mag!"

Like the gusts catching her wings, her mumbo's imploring words seemed to give Perilous a sudden lift. She rustled her wings as if to shake off any doubt – or that unfamiliar, awful feeling called *anger* that had gripped her. But she still suspected there was something her pair wasn't telling them.

She fixed her eyes on the horizon. "I hope they know what they're doing, Rampant, that Council of yours," she said, "because I'm not at all sure *you* do."

Rampant didn't reply. Instead he spread his wings, and felt the wind lift him. Then he roared, "IN THE NAME OF FLAME – TAKE OFF!"

He launched himself from the crag and they followed, swooping at first, then rising.

CHAPTER 9

The next time the family landed, it was on a clifftop high above the shore. Apart from a narrow strip of sand, the water was right below them, and seemed to stretch away for ever.

"Now," said Rampant, catching his breath, "we'll rest here for a dark, then we'll be on our way."

"Over *that*," said Perilous, gazing out at the vast grey expanse and feeling her think-space filling with all kinds of dreadful gnawing thinks.

"That's right. And the Council will know we did our duty."

Perilous turned to him. "How will they know, Rampant – your precious Council? How could they possibly? There's no way to signal that far."

The black dragon stood still, wing-tips quivering.

"When we've completed our mission, we'll report back," he said. "And the quicker the better."

Red wasn't listening. His think-space was elsewhere. He gazed out at the expanse of water, and now, quite unexpectedly, he felt something for the first time. One of those *feelings* that his teacher had told them dragons didn't have good words for.

A think now hit him – more strongly even than any gust of wind – that he couldn't make it: not over that endless flat grey expanse. He just *couldn't*. There was no land as far as he could see. Who knew if there was any, anywhere but here? He wanted so much to beg his dag to turn back, back to the comfort of cave; but before he could say anything, his mag, trailing a thin stream of angry – yes, *angry!* – brown smoke, shuffled close to him. She put her wing over her mumbo.

"I've changed my think-space," she said calmly. "I'm taking you home."

There was a pause. Then Rampant said, "There's no going back. Not until we've found them."

"Found who?" said his pair, without looking at him.

"Uprights."

Perilous didn't say anything for a moment. She just stood there, taking it in. It was as if the word *upright* had to burrow very slowly, like some creeping-crawling horrible *thing*, into her think-space. She turned to her pair very slowly.

"You'd better not have just said *uprights*, Rampant. You'd better not."

There was another awkward pause. Rampant shuffled uncomfortably on the cliff edge.

"The Council—"

"No."

"The Council said—"

"Don't tell me."

"—that there just might be—"

"*Might?*"

"Yes. Somewhere out there in the Endless Water…"

"What, Rampant? WHAT?"

"Land-lumps. They said – they *suspect* – that there just may have been a few uprights who survived. And if they did—"

"That's a very small *if*," Perilous put in.

"—then we might find them. We *must* find them."

"And then what? What if we do find them? What then?"

"We'll have a heads-together. And ask for" – Rampant could hardly say it – "their help."

"Uprights HELP us? Why would they help *us*?

Why would they do something like that, Rampant? After what we did!"

Rampant's voice deepened to a growl. "What? Tell me – what did *we* do?"

"WE RIP-BURN-KILLED THEM! We destroyed their homes! We" – she glanced at her son, who was staring wildly back at her, and lowered her voice – "we drove them away!"

"After what they did to us – to *everything*! We had no choice. Just like now – we have no choice!"

Later that dark, after fire-out, the family was gathered again on the clifftop. They'd found a large rock to crouch behind, which helped take the bite out of the wind. Just as Red was finally falling asleep, and thinks, like the waves he'd seen on the beach that light, were washing into his think-space, he realized that despite the fear, despite the unknown, he *did* want to go on. He *did* want to find uprights.

He overheard his dag say to his mag, "We've tried everything, believe me. The Council sent searchers out to look for coal far beyond the normal live-space boundaries into the Old Time places. They found a few coal stacks, scattered about, but we've used those up too. The tail-point is, uprights caused the coal we've been using all this time. They may know where more of it is, or at least how to cause more of it."

At this, Red sat up against the rock. "Dag," he said, yawning, "what happens if we don't find them – the uprights, I mean? What if we don't ... if it's just too far? If there are no survivors?"

Perilous looked at her pair, her eyes beseeching. "Yes, Rampant, what then?"

Rampant didn't answer. He just crouched there, gazing out at the almost black undulating mass below him, the dark-shine reflected on its surface, causing what appeared to be a pale path stretching from the sand to the horizon. Rampant secretly wished he could jump the rest of the way on it.

He lowered his head and drew the Block of Knowledge out of his pouch with his teeth.

"The block!" exclaimed Red. "What are you going to do with it, Dag?"

"I'm not going to do *anything* with it. I'm just going to give it to them."

"We have to find them first," snorted Perilous. She looked out over the Endless Water and watched the sky-flappers wheeling and calling, their white wings flashing in the dark-shine. She longed to be as free as they were.

Then her thinks drifted – back to the Council, to their so-called wisdom in which her pair had put all his trust, and for whom he had done the unthinkable: lied to her and risked bringing their son. And suddenly, strangely, she saw the dragonsense in it, in the duty, in the mission, in risking everything; and hope crept back into her think-space – hope enough for all of them. She turned to Rampant.

"We have a mission," she said firmly. "At light-up, we leave."

With a little excited bark, Red jumped to his feet and clacked his wings.

"Yes!" he cried. "We're going – WE'RE REALLY GOING!"

BLOCK IV
MEETING THE
UPRIGHTS

CHAPTER 10

Almost as soon as the light-shine appeared on the horizon, the three dragons lined up at the edge of the Endless Water. Rampant pulled the Block of Knowledge once again out of his pouch. With his tongue, he carefully turned the top part of it – the *hard* part – over. Now Red could see that what he'd presumed was a solid block was, in fact, divided into many very thin things like … leaves? Some of them had colours on them. Most were covered in black streaks.

"The Council told me those marks are like smoke signals," said Rampant, his voice uncertain.

As he looked through the leaves, Perilous stood with her back to the Endless Water, taking deep breaths and letting worry-smoke drift revealingly from her nostrils. So neither of them noticed the remarkable thing that had caught their son's attention.

Far across the water, something appeared to be moving towards them.

"Mag! Dag! Look – out there!"

Red pointed his tail so hard it nearly tipped him tail-end over horns. His parents turned. At first they couldn't see anything – dragon eyesight isn't too sharp at the best of times, and the salty spray blowing in from the Endless Water was making it even more difficult. A dragon's sense of smell is far better, but that was no use either: it was still too far away, no more than a tiny thing appearing and disappearing with the rise and fall of the waves.

Red kept jumping up and down and pointing. Finally his mag and dag saw it.

"What is that?" asked Rampant, craning his neck. "A bit of land?"

"Of course not; it's moving," said Perilous. "And it's coming this way."

The dragon family stood for what seemed like a whole dark and light, staring and staring out at it, each of their think-spaces full of questions. But it wasn't until the thing was much closer that they could finally make out what it was. At least, what it appeared to be.

"It's a big piece of tree," said Red disappointedly, "and it's got a long hole along the top with living things in."

"What kind of living things?" asked his dag.

They looked again. Suddenly Perilous's voice broke the claw-tightening silence with just a tiny whisper. "*Uprights…*"

"Uprights!" growled Rampant. "They can't be. If there *are* any – and I have my doubts – then they're out *there* somewhere, where they belong. But come here – to our mainland? They wouldn't DARE!" Dark, threatening smoke drifted from his nostrils.

"They're uprights; I just know it!" his pair repeated. "FLY FOR YOUR LIVES!"

Rampant threw himself in front of Perilous and blew some pale, calming smoke at her.

"No," he said. "We've always been much bigger and stronger than them – now we're cleverer, too. We have nothing to fear from uprights. Don't you see: if they're here, it saves us a journey. It's what you wanted!"

As the floating thing drew nearer, the dragons took a few cautious steps back from where the water met the land. Red was first to speak.

"Dag, that's not just a big piece of tree, is it?"

"No, son. I think it's a wet-floater."

"A what?"

"My dag found a piece of one once, *long* ago, when he was far from cave searching for coal stacks. It was by a big-wet, near some abandoned upright live-space. He flew with it back to cave—"

"*Trappings in cave, results will be grave,*" whispered Red. "Your dag broke the—"

"I know. The old dragon used to sneak things back all the time. He showed me his piece of that wet-floater. Told me uprights might've used them to escape the Great Ridding. Then, to scare me, he said, *some day they'll be back.*"

Rampant blew out a cloud of dark smoke that floated in the air briefly before being whisked away on a gust of wind.

"My dag said, when that happens – and it *will* happen – dragons must be ready."

"Ready to do what, Dag?"

"Whatever they have to do to keep them away."

CHAPTER 11

They stood there, the three dragons with their backs to the cliff, clear against its whiteness, waiting for the wet-floater to arrive, and for the uprights, their old enemies, to do whatever uprights do.

Would they agree to a civilized heads-together? Or would they, far more likely, start a fight?

"Now," said Red's dag, making himself as tall as he could, "whatever happens next, we must show them we're better than they are."

"How, Dag?"

"By being polite … and decent."

"Is there so much as a wisp in the Trail of Smoke about an upright being those things to a dragon?" asked Perilous. "Maybe they'll take our politeness and decency for weakness."

Since they'd been in that town-place, Red had some idea of what an upright might look like. But their size still worried him. The ones they'd seen on the walls were much smaller than a dragon, but the solid ones that stood on the stone blocks were bigger. And they had hard pointed things for... He didn't want to think!

Questions without answers made his think-space tingle.

As the wet-floater came nearer, Red could see that it was caused by something tree-like and had stick-things hanging out of it on either side. The uprights caused them to move – forwards and backwards – and that's what seemed to pull them through the water.

And then Red got a real shock. The uprights were only half the size he'd expected, and their faces were covered in fur! The wet-floater reached the shallows, and the stick-pullers turned around, and Red realized he'd only been seeing the back of them, and that a large part of them had been hidden altogether.

The moment the uprights saw the dragons, they seemed to lose all control, yelling and pointing. Two of them stood up, swayed and fell out of the wet-floater, making it rock wildly. Others jumped out and started frantically pushing it, as fast as they could, back out into the Endless Water. Another disappeared briefly then reappeared holding a different sort of stick. He pointed it at the three dragons standing on the shore showing their teeth politely in welcome. Suddenly—

CACK-ACK!

Something that sounded a lot like a furry-buzzer flew past Red's ear. He heard his dag let out a roar and, next thing he knew, his mag had pulled him to the ground and thrown herself on top of him, squeezing the smoke out of him. Taking shallow breaths, he peeped out from beneath her chest just in time to see Rampant reach the edge of the water in three giant jumps. Even from his back, Red could tell his dag was angry – no, worse!

The massive full-grown waded into the water without fear, put his snout under the pointed part of the wet-floater and tilted it, flipping it right over. Uprights tumbled out into the water, yelling and waving their four long thin legs. The massive black dragon backed to the water's edge, dragging the upside-down wet-floater with his tail hooked under the front. Then he stood, chest heaving, front paws firmly across his chest, staring at the uprights floundering in the shallows.

"I don't think Dag is being polite," Red said to his mag.

"Why should he be," she retorted, snapping her teeth menacingly, "when *they* weren't?" She stood, lifted Red onto his haunches, and blew the sand off him. "Now stay right here." She moved to the water's edge to stand, claw-to-claw, with her pair.

Red stared with fascination at the uprights flailing in the water. He noticed several retrieving their pulling-sticks and waving them in a way that suggested they might like to hit his mag and dag with them. He gave a little angry huff but was distracted by something he noticed further along the shore: one of *them*, moving like any ordinary animal on four legs, was crawling out of the water, up onto the sand.

Red felt something like a wave surge over him and wash away his fear. It was curiosity. Before he realized what he was doing, he was jumping over to take a closer look.

Red could see that this upright was very small – a young one, perhaps? He felt much more curious than scared of it.

Then it got to its back feet and stood upright!

He could see clearly now that it was shorter than

he was, and had four long straight legs. No wings. No horns. No scales. And – unless it was very short – no tail. Its skin was several colours, and the water seemed to have soaked right into it and made it heavy. It stood before him, dripping, with its head-fur matted over its face, two eyes staring wildly, and its front legs hanging at its sides.

Suddenly Red thought of something: its *hands*!

Now was his chance to see hands – real ones, not a look-like. Bravely he jumped closer and said, as politely as he could, "Hello." He was also careful to give it a friendly signal, breathing the whitest smoke he could produce in little puffs.

The upright stared at him with its mouth hanging open. Then it spoke! And in words he could understand but hardly hear.

"You're *red*!" it said. And then louder, "You're red … a real, living, breathing *red* dragon!" It took a step closer and stopped. "You're not – no, how could you be? – *the* Red Dragon, I mean, the one in the song?"

Red stared blankly. He didn't know what a *song* was. He didn't know if he should be speaking to an upright at all. The little upright began to speak in a funny way, making a noise a bit like a sky-flapper.

*"When the Red Red Dragon comes out of the sky,
I know that I will learn how to fly. When the Red Red
Dragon comes over the sea, what a world that will
be for him and for me..."* It stopped warbling then,
and said in a plain voice, "Well? Are you? *The* Red
Dragon?"

Red didn't know how to answer. So he just shuffled
a little closer and said, "Do you have ... *hand*?"

It gave him a funny look. "You mean do I have
a hand? Of course I do. As a matter of fact, I have two.
Look." It held up its front paws to show him. Only
they weren't paws; they were bare and flat and pink
with long wormy things hanging off them. Nothing
like claws.

Red did what all dragons do when they want to
explore something new. First he sniffed one of them –
it smelled of the Endless Water. There was something
else, quite delicious but at the same time scary. An
upright smell?

"You smell good enough to eat."

The upright gave a frightened little gasp and backed
away.

"What's wrong?" asked Red.

"Don't you know it's not nice to tell someone you

want to eat them, especially if you've got great big jaws and teeth?"

"Oh! No! I don't want to *eat* eat you. I just want to…" He whipped his tongue out and licked one of the hands. The upright snatched it away.

"What are you *doing*?" it hissed.

"Tasting…"

"Tasting what?"

"Your *hand*." Again the long curious tongue stretched out and this time touched the wet skin of the upright's chest. "Why's your skin different colours?"

"My…? That's not skin! That's wool – my wool sweater."

His tongue touched the *sweater* (lovely new word, he thought) again.

"Stop!" it squealed.

"Why do you cover yourself in … *wool*?" asked Red. "What's wrong with your own skin?"

"Nothing. Unless it's cold. But you can't just run around with nothing on, can you?"

"I do," said Red proudly.

The upright looked the dragon up and down. "We don't have scales like you. Can I touch them?"

The thought of an upright touching him gave Red

the shivers. Nevertheless, he understood that having sniffed and licked its wool, it was only polite.

"If you must," he said stiffly.

The upright came closer, reached out its hand and gently stroked Red's tummy. There were no scales there, but it was the closest bit of him.

"You feel *cool*," it said, sounding surprised.

Red said nothing. He was too absorbed by the strange, warm, very pleasant feeling of the hand stroking him.

"A red dragon," it said again, as if it couldn't believe it. The upright began to make that strange warbling sound again: "*When the Red Red Dragon comes over the hill, I know he will come to heal, not to kill—*"

"Why d'you keep causing noises like that?"

"What? You mean singing?"

"Dragons don't do *sing-ging*."

"That's so sad!" It kept stroking Red's belly and causing tingly thinks in his think-space. "You know, I always thought you'd be more scaly."

"I am."

He turned sideways and let the upright stroke the smooth hard red scales on his back. It made his tail twitch. He turned round again.

"Could you cause something – with the hand?"

"*Cause* something?"

"Yes – show me the power."

The upright gave him a funny look. "What power? I don't understand."

"Maybe" – Red looked around – "pick something up, like … *that* little thing, by your other hand."

The upright looked down at the ground. "That's not a hand, silly – that's my foot!"

It bent down, and Red watched, enthralled, as it

used the Power of the Hand to pick up a tiny round hard thing by its foot.

"Look," it said, holding out its hand and showing him. "Go ahead. Take it."

"Oooh!" said Red excitedly, not knowing what it was. "Would you drop it in my pouch?" He pulled it open with his side-claw.

The upright peered at it. "Wow! You have a pocket!"

And before Red could stop it, the upright thrust its hand down into the skinny depths.

"Don't do that!" Red growled, and he let out a puff of grey warning-smoke. "That's rude!"

The upright, shocked by his reaction, snatched its hand out. "Sorry!"

Dragonsense quickly returned, and Red huffed and shook himself. "It's all right," he said. "You didn't know."

After a moment, the hand was opened to reveal a small lump of coal. The upright gazed at it. "Why're you carrying this around?"

"It's mine – put it back," Red said firmly.

The hand closed and was pulled away. "Just tell me."

There was a pause while Red considered if he should answer. But there was something about this little upright – despite all that he'd ever heard about them – that put him at ease.

"We need it," he muttered.

"What for?" it asked, turning the coal in its long pink – what *were* those things?

Red was still feeling a bit angry at the intrusion into his pouch. Without thinking, he tried to snatch back his piece of coal. His head moved as fast as a snake striking. By mistake he caught one of the long pink wormy things between his teeth and—

"OW! Why'd you bite me?"

Bite! No! NO! That was a terrible, *terrible* word – the worst! Dragons don't do biting – unless of course they're hunting. And he wasn't hunting, was he? He was just trying to…

"Sorry!" he stammered. "I'm so sorry! I didn't mean to. I just wanted my—"

There was a sudden uprush of noise along the water's edge.

They both turned to look. The two full-growns had been holding some sort of heads-together with the uprights, but, by the looks of things, the time for heads-together had ended and the time for heads-bitten-off had begun!

Red's mag and dag were standing at the water's edge, long necks stretched, huge jaws open showing their teeth, spreading their wings and flapping them so hard that they sent clouds of fine sand flying everywhere.

Still standing in the shallows, the uprights – who had clearly got the shock of their lives – started attacking Rampant with their pulling-sticks, swinging them about, while he batted them away like twigs with his mighty tail, and his pair did the same with hers.

"Back! Get back, you MONSTER!" one of them shrieked, poking frantically with its pulling-stick.

"LIKE – I – KEEP – SAYING!" roared Rampant, smashing another pulling-stick. "WE – JUST – WANT – TO – TALK!"

"Mag and Dag can *fight*…" Red whispered under his breath, and he felt a hot, tingling sensation behind his eyes.

Just as he was wondering if he ought to go and help, one of the uprights spotted them. At once it dropped its stick and came pounding towards them.

"That's my dad," said the little upright. "I'd better go." But it lingered. "Do dragons have names?"

"Of course we do. Mine is Red."

"I should have guessed. Don't you want to know mine?"

"Uprights have *names*?" said Red, unable to hide his surprise.

"Uprights? What's an upright?"

"*You're* an upright."

"Oooh. You mean that's your word for *humans* – and yes, we have names. I'm Lou."

"*Loooooouuuu.*"

"Bye, Red." Lou made a move to leave, then stopped, and came back. It held out a hand. "Sorry," it said, "I almost forgot to give this back." It was the bit of coal.

"Just leave it on the sand."

Lou did as he asked, and he lowered his snout, snatched it up in his teeth and stuffed it back in his pouch just as—

"Lou! Lou! GET AWAY FROM THAT – THAT *THING*!"

It was Lou's *dad*. The full-grown upright had stopped running now and was standing just beyond reach, flinging his front legs around frantically.

"I'd really better go. Bye!" Lou gave Red a little wave with its hand, and scampered away.

Red watched with interest the way it moved: on two legs, swiftly, and without jumping. It reminded him of a ground-flapper fleeing from the threat of life-over. He'd often seen this when his mag was hunting. It bothered him when a think came that perhaps Lou was fleeing from *him*. But far more disturbing was another creeping feeling that there was no dragon word for.

A feeling that he wished the little upright hadn't left him quite so soon.

CHAPTER 12

The uprights were leaving. They'd turned their wet-floater over and were scrambling, as fast as they could, back into it. Red watched Lou being picked up by what looked like another full-grown. It turned and flapped its hand at him, and he lifted one paw uncertainly.

"*Bye!*"

Two of the bigger uprights pushed the wet-floater away from the shore, while the others tugged furiously on the pulling-sticks, and soon it was heading back out into the Endless Water.

Red could see Lou staring back at him, and he felt a stirring. He shook himself and jumped back along the sand to where his parents were standing, out of breath and still furious.

"EXACTLY what I expected," his dag growled, blowing out a big cloud of dark smoke.

"What did they say, Dag?"

"You mean when they weren't whacking me with those pull-things?" He gave his sore tail a painful flick. "Nothing decent. I tried to talk to them – to be reasonable. I asked where they were from and what they were doing here, on *our* mainland."

"What about the heads-together?"

"Heads-*apart*, more like."

"Outrageous! Simply *outrageous*!" put in Perilous, flapping her wings angrily. "I've never seen anything so rude in all my dragon lights. Your granddag was right: they're disgusting creatures, not fit for a heads-together, let alone a *world* together!"

All three of them watched the wet-floater pull away. And they all felt a deep sense of relief.

"They called me a monster," murmured Rampant.

"What's that?" asked Red.

"It's not good," replied his mag. "Your dag blew only white smoke at them; offered them nothing but decency, even when they were trying to…" Her voice cracked, and she couldn't go on for a moment. "Even when they were trying to hurt him."

"Did they hurt you, Dag?"

"Look at him – look at his shoulder. Just look what they did!"

Red peered at his dag's mighty shoulder and noticed a little hole, with a trickle of red-wet oozing from it.

Rampant shrugged off the pain with a quick shake. "Lucky it just hit my scales."

Perilous touched the broken scale with her tongue and found, to her amazement, something lodged in there. She sniffed then probed it. "Ugh!" She gave it a little squeeze with her teeth. It popped out and she spat it on the sand.

Red bent down to look. "What is it?"

"Whatever it is, I hope I never feel it again."

Red peered back out at the wet-floater with a feeling of disbelief – and, despite himself, a nagging sense of wonderment.

"Did you see the little one – the one I was talking to?"

His mag and dag turned to him quickly.

"You were *talking* to it?" Perilous gasped.

"Yes. And it had a name."

"A *name*? Uprights have *names*?"

"This one does. It's Lou."

His mag and dag exchanged puzzled looks.

"If it talked," said Rampant, "did it tell you why they had come?"

Red shook his head.

"I can't understand why they'd take the risk," mused Perilous. "They know we're here, that this place belongs to us, that it's against the law."

"*Our* law, not theirs," Red pointed out.

"If they know all that," said Rampant, "then they

must have a very good reason. And if they came once, then—"

"—they might come again," said his pair.

Red's ears perked up. "Why don't we wait for them?"

"You mean as prey? I couldn't bring myself to hunt one those *pathetic* creatures."

"I don't mean to rip-burn-kill, Mag. I mean to try again – to talk. If we catch one, we might be able to convince them that we're decent, and ask for their help."

"Son? The Council was right about you." Rampant turned and scanned the cliff-face. "First thing we must do is find a cave."

CHAPTER 13

After jumping a short distance, the dragons came to an inlet.

"See if you can find something suitable here," Red's mag told him. "We'll fly across and take a look on the far side."

Only a short time after that, Red made a discovery – the perfect cave!

It was exactly the right depth and height. Best of all it couldn't be seen from the Endless Water because it faced across the inlet. There was plenty of driftwood outside too for a good cave fire. Red explored inside.

There were some strange things in the back – like big chunks of wood – but he didn't bother with those. Without further ado, he jumped out of the cave and flew to where his dag was toiling along, searching in vain along the rugged but caveless cliff.

"Dag! DAG!"

"What is it, son?"

"I've found one!"

Rampant hurried back with him to inspect the place. He lingered a little over the chunks of wood in the back, but he didn't want to find anything wrong with the wonderful live-space. After patting Red praisingly, he jumped round the end of the inlet and fetched his pair.

Soon the family was settled in the cave with a nice, comforting fire lit by Perilous's flaming breath. The only trouble was that they had nothing to eat. Famished, Red set off to explore.

He jumped along the sand to the top of the inlet, where he found pools among some low rocks. A movement in one of them made him look down, and he saw strange things, all different colours, moving about in the water. Without thinking, he darted his snout straight down into the pool and grabbed one with his teeth. He got an awful fright when – WHOOSH! – the water went up his nose. There was a deep hissing in his chest as it hit his fire.

He snatched his snout out and blew hard through his nose to clear it. Instead of smoke, steam streamed out of his nostrils. It felt horrible, and he dropped the thing he'd caught onto the sand while he recovered, taking short, hard breaths to keep his chest-fire alight. Water didn't normally put a dragon's fire out but this time it had gone down into the wrong stomach. Red gave his head a big shake, then looked around.

The thing he'd caught was still flapping wildly in the sand. Soon the flapping slowed, then stopped altogether, until it lay still. Red sniffed it, then explored with his tongue. It smelled and tasted very strange – but good.

Next thing he knew, he was eating it. The bones were sharp, and Red had to crunch them up carefully before swallowing – delicious! Now what?

He investigated the pool again. There were more

of the strange but tasty flappy-things – except they didn't flap in the water; they seemed to move almost effortlessly. But to get them, he'd have to put his face in the water again and risk having that horrible losing-fire feeling. Then he realized: if he closed his nostrils and didn't breathe in through his mouth, he'd be able to grab more, and take them back to cave. Dragons must be able to close their nostrils, which are on top of their snouts, to stop rain getting in. Red moved from pool to pool, snatching as many as he could, and popping them in his pouch, where they flapped and tickled and then lay still. This made him uneasy. He'd helped his mag hunt before, of course, but he'd still not got used to causing life-over.

When Red jumped back to their cave, his pouch was bulging with his new food that he decided to call *sand-flappers*. He showed them to his mag and dag, who were rather doubtful at first, but when he persuaded them to have a taste, they quickly changed their think-spaces.

"You sure this isn't meat?" asked his dag suspiciously.

"Meat has legs, doesn't it, Dag?" said Red, relishing every fleshy morsel.

"If it's meat, it's not like any I've ever tasted," said Perilous, enjoying it nevertheless.

"Well," said Rampant, taking a big bite, "if we're staying here, we'll need to find more of them!"

The family feasted till their stomachs were full, swallowed a little coal to fuel their chest-fires, then huddled by the fire and slept, as all dragons do, deeply and without dreams.

CHAPTER 14

The family lost count of the darks and lights that passed while they waited to put Red's plan into action. During that time, they stuffed themselves with sand-flappers. Perilous, always on the hunt, managed to catch plenty of fur-hoppers and sky-flappers and, one time, much to everyone's surprise, a large hoof-runner.

"There it was, right below me!" Perilous said proudly around the fire one dark, tearing off a chunk of meat and gulping it down. "I stalked it – high above so it couldn't see me – then, as soon as it wandered into the open I just—"

"Swooped down for the rip-burn-kill!" put in Red excitedly. No one seemed to mind him saying that any more. They didn't mind him saying a lot of things.

Perilous made the cave more comfortable by dragging in soft greenery for them to sleep on, while Rampant became a dab paw at sand-flapper catching.

He learned to stand belly-deep in the water and plunge his head under with lightning swiftness – "Good one, Dag!" – pulling out flapper after flapper and tossing them onto the sand with a flick of his neck. He ate them contentedly and told himself that he was still a green-feeder by munching up some Endless Water weed-stuff he found to go with it.

Rampant arranged for each of them to take turns on watch on the top of the cliff, because like Granddag always said, they had to be ready. Taking off from the shore was always difficult. They had to jump fast along the sand to work up speed, use their strong shoulder muscles to flap their wings for take-off, then circle upward. This involved flying short distances over water. Red was lighter and more agile than the full-growns, and so could take off more easily.

After a couple of lights, he suggested that he should do most of the watching.

"You?" said his dag snortily. "Up there alone? Staring down at the Endless Water? Bah! You'll end of boredom!"

"It's not boring if it's part of the mission, Dag."

His mag and dag looked at each other. Both felt a rush of pride that their mumbo – now a half-grown –

had got his think-space round such a dragonly think.

"Make sure you eat up there, Ferocity," said his mag. "You'll find plenty of fur-hoppers – easy to catch, easy to swallow. If you see something bigger, tail-signal me. Oh, and don't forget to eat your coal!"

Left on his own at the top of the cliff, Red was soon reminded that he wasn't much of a hunter. Even when he saw something he was supposed to end, he could never quite manage more than a cloud of white smoke and a harmless poke with his snout.

Once, he managed to chase and grab a fur-hopper between his teeth, but its little legs kicking wildly against his chin tickled and made him feel sorry for it, and he let it go. He stopped his hunger by eating green-stuff, which grew all around. And he was very careful to eat his daily ration of coal and he practised smoke signals – just to keep in touch with his mag and dag below.

Sometimes, while on watch, he did get bored, crouched up there all alone, staring and staring at the endless wet sameness, and then his think-space would fill to bursting with uprights and fighting and the wet-floater and Lou … always Lou, the little one who did that weird *singing*-thing and seemed to think he was *the* Red Dragon.

What did she mean by that?

At other times, something would grab his attention – an object out there on the waves; something that might just be *them*. When that happened, he'd jump up, rush over to the edge of the cliff and gaze out with eyes half closed to see better. But always he'd realize, on closer inspection, that it was nothing – just a trick of the light-shine. He could feel himself torn between excitement that Lou might return, and relief that the rest of them – full-growns wielding painful pulling-sticks – hadn't come back to hurt his family.

Darks and lights passed. Still no sign of the uprights.

Red's mag and dag were becoming more and more agitated, especially his mag, who complained bitterly that the Council had sent them on an *impossible* mission. They kept watch, stuffed their bellies, slept their dreamless sleeps, lit fires, and kept watch some more. But hope, like the light-shine on an unbroken horizon, began to fade. Up on his clifftop perch, Red's thinks drifted again to the uprights.

He thought about the look-likes hanging on the wall, and other wondrous things he's seen in the town-place. He closed his eyes to back-think and could see the big stone upright that was going to end the dragon curled at its feet. Suddenly they weren't stone any more; they were fighting…

The upright raised its terrible pointed stick, the dragon writhed at its feet, lashing its barbed tail. Red leaped forward and sank his teeth into the brute upright's leg! It let out an agonized howl, then turned on him. The *other* dragon reared up on its back legs and grabbed the upright by the throat, using its claws to tear flesh until the red-wet flowed. Red dragged the upright off the stone block, and soon all three were struggling on the ground, writhing, and tearing and biting and roaring when—

A guilty feeling made Red's eyes snap open.

It was as well it did, because if he'd kept back-thinking, he might have missed what he'd waited so very long to see.

A wet-floater. And it was heading straight towards him!

BLOCK V
THE UPRIGHTS
RETURN

CHAPTER 15

Red stared at the wet-floater for a long moment,
almost forgetting to breathe. This one was bigger,
a different shape, and it moved by something else –
a sort of large white *wing*?

While Red watched, too fascinated to move, the big
wet-floater stopped, and a smaller one – like the one
that had come before – was dropped into the water.
Uprights climbed down into it and began to pull.

Suddenly the plan came back into Red's think-space.

He rushed to the cliff edge, where a large boulder
was waiting, and shouldered it over the edge. Craning
his neck, he watched it tumble down the rocky face
until it hit the sand below with a heavy THUMP!
A moment later, his dag came jumping out of their
cave, looked up excitedly, and sent a tail-signal
acknowledging the warning. The next signal ordered,
Stay where you are!

What? Up here? And miss all the fun? Red, pretending he hadn't seen it, spread his wings and launched himself off the cliff, curving downward and landing with a string of little jumps at his dag's feet.

"I told you to stay up there!"

"Did you? Sorry, Dag, I'd already taken off."

"A likely dragon story! Now get your tail-end back up there at once! There may be fighting."

Red made a move to leave, then stopped. "What's the plan, Dag?"

His dag gave him a funny look. "The *plan*?"

"You do have a plan, don't you?"

"Of course! Of course I have one."

"What is it?"

Rampant gave a little cough. "Well ... er ... the plan is to – to hide."

"Hide?"

"Yes, at first, and then ... er ... when they come to cave, you know, grab one of them."

"*That's* your plan?"

"What's wrong with it?"

"First of all, how d'you know they'll even *come* to cave? I mean, they might not. They might go somewhere else. They might just stay on the beach."

There was an awkward pause. Rampant gave an agitated huff.

"They'll come, all right. They'll come for those big lumps of wood at the back. Those things stink of flaming uprights. And when they do, we'll grab one and ... and the rest will run away."

"What if they *don't* run away? What if they stay and fight? What if they've got one of those stick-things that sends furry-buzzers to make more holes in your scales?"

"THEN THEY'LL FEEL MY FIRE!" growled Perilous, emerging from cave.

Rampant's expression changed. His bright green eyes flashed. Red froze. His mag and dag were out of sight of the uprights, where the inlet started, with just their heads jutting around the cliff, peering at the small wet-floater, which was coming nearer.

What if *Lou* was in it? What if...?

A think flashed through Red's think-space of his mag opening her great jaws and sinking her teeth into upright flesh – *Lou*'s flesh!

"NO!" he blurted.

132

"Quiet!" hissed his mag.

"Listen to me! Please wait!" Red jumped urgently in front of them.

"Ferocity!" snorted Perilous, puffing out hot, angry smoke. "I won't tell you again. Go back to cave NOW!"

"Are you going to be polite or – or violent?" Red wanted to know.

"We'll be whatever we need to be," warned his dag, rubbing his chin against the wound on his shoulder where the uprights had caused the hole.

"Please, Dag, *please* don't…"

His mag curled her neck around his and hiked him backwards. "Do as you're told, Ferocity!" she ordered. "Or I'll give your tail-end such a scorching you won't be able to crouch for lights!"

Red had never had a scorched tail-end, and had no desire to find out what it felt like, so he jumped slowly back into cave and found a dark place at the back to hide. Yet he couldn't help thinking that if he stayed here, he'd miss the fighting, and something bad might happen to Lou – *if* it had come back.

He was just going to sneak out again when his gaze fell on the big chunks of wood. Distracted, he sniffed at one and put his eye to a crack. He could tell they weren't solid, and that there were things inside them. But he couldn't tell what. He was surprised his dag hadn't broken them open by now; he could have done it easily.

While he was wondering what might be inside the chunks, his mag and dag came bounding in.

"They're coming! They're COMING!" hissed Perilous.

Rampant kicked sand over the remains of the fire, noticing only then – and feeling very unclever for not having noticed before – that there'd been another fire under theirs.

"I *knew* it," he whispered.

Perilous said nothing. She just swept burned wood-ends and paw prints away with her tail. Then she jumped to the back of the cave, and before Red knew what was happening, she'd thrust him behind the wooden lumps and squeezed in beside him.

"Not a sound!" she whispered urgently.

Rampant crouched in a dark hollow at the back of the cave, becoming still as a shadow. They could hear chattering voices.

And they were coming closer.

CHAPTER 16

Red pricked his ears to hear if Lou was among the uprights entering the cave. Yes … YES! Its higher voice was recognizable among the other, deeper ones. Red was glad and fearful and excited all at the same time. He had a strange think: why would Lou's dag bring it if there was danger? But then another came. *My* dag brought *me* because I have a good think-space. Maybe Lou has a good think-space too?

Now light was flickering across the sides and top of the cave: firelight.

Red tried to peep round the side of the block. His mag put a heavy paw on his head and pulled him back, but not before he'd caught a glimpse of a group of uprights – Lou among them – in the mouth of the cave, carrying more sticks, short ones this time, with fire on the ends of them. He kept still and listened.

"There's a funny smell in here!"

"Yeah, smoke."

"Must be those dragons – filthy scavengers!"

"What if they're still here?"

"No chance. We'd have seen 'em by now, especially that weird little red one."

"Still can't believe it – a *red* dragon! Gives me the shivers just thinking about it."

"I told you to shoot it! Why didn't you – right between the eyes!"

From his hiding place behind the blocks, their words hit Red like furry-buzzer bites. Why were they talking about him like that? It wasn't decent!

Then he heard Lou speak. "I talked to it," it said calmly.

The chatter stopped. Then another voice, breathless and accusing. "What for?"

"It talked to me."

"*Talked*, was it? Roared, more like. They stole our lands, and they stole our words!"

"Why even bother? They've nothing to say. Nothing worth hearing, anyway."

Without meaning to, Rampant let out a tiny growl in the blackness. The uprights froze.

"What was that? I heard something!"

There was a pause while they listened. The dragons held their breaths.

"You're getting paranoid, lad. There's always noises in here – probably just an echo." And the upright made a WHOOOO! sound that bounced off the walls. "See?"

A quieter voice emerged. Lou's dag. "You talked to it? Face to face? But I thought you said it bit you."

"Nipped," said Lou. "Anyway, it was an accident."

"Freak of nature, you mean! The whole fire-breathing lot of 'em!"

The voices and the tramp of feet were heading towards the back of the cave. Now, Red thought, his dag would pounce and there'd be a fight! He took a deep breath and felt the fire in his chest glow, and a hotness behind his eyes.

But Rampant stayed where he was, in the shadow. Unseen and unheard.

"Before we get to work on these crates," said Lou's dag, "let's make a proper fire, cook up some food."

Near the cave mouth, the uprights gathered some driftwood and made a fire, exactly where the dragons had made theirs, and soon delicious smells – quite unfamiliar to the dragons – wafted to the back. Red realized his tongue was hanging out, and dripping. He sucked it in – *SHLOOP!* – and his mag gave him a sharp nudge.

"I'm sure I heard something! Anyone else?"

There was a listening silence around the fire.

"You *are* getting paranoid, lad."

"You can never be too careful. Not on the mainland."

The group went back to talking. Red strained his ears to pick out Lou's voice. Every now and then he could hear it. He was glad the little upright was there.

"Someone's got to go," said one of the deep-voiced uprights.

"Not me. Not after the last time."

"That was an accident – no big deal."

"I broke my leg!"

"What's a broken leg when you found that cellar? All those tools and tins of food!"

There was a whoop of approval from the others.

"Lucky you weren't there when I opened the pork and beans! Ugh! Stank the place out!"

"What d'you expect after sitting there for a hundred years?"

"Little of all we value here wakes on the morn of its hundredth year without both feeling and … smelling queer."

They all cackled.

"Anyway, you found *oil*, didn't you?" said Lou suddenly.

"Enough to fill a bath. Got us through winter, that's for sure." It was that quieter voice again.

"It's books we're after this time – more precious than oil."

Red pricked up his ears till the tips met behind his horns: what could *books* be?

"Enough talk. What we need to do is find a way to get inland – new territory – and look there. We just need to find a way past those stinking dragons!"

There was a silence. Red felt his mag, crouched beside him, stiffen. Her big, sensitive ears had caught a sound: small bare feet padding across the stone floor. Moments later, Red could smell it.

Lou had left the others and was walking quietly towards the back of the cave.

"Where're you going, girl?" came an anxious voice.

"Just thought I'd check the crates."

There was a scrabbling sound, and the next moment, Lou's hand appeared over the top of the blocks behind which Red and his mag were hiding. They cowered lower. Suddenly and shockingly, Lou's head popped over the top.

For a smoke-stopping moment, Perilous and the upright stared at each other.

Lou's blue eyes were almost as big as the full-grown's green ones, and its mouth was open. Red felt his mag make a jerky movement as if to seize Lou, but instead she simply allowed a trickle of dark, threatening smoke to leave one nostril. A warning signal that no dragon could have mistaken.

Red, crouching between his mag's haunches, reached his tail over his head and gently touched the wormy things that were gripping the top edge of the wood. He made the tiniest *shushing* sound through his back teeth. Lou hung there, just above them…

Then a voice came from the fireside: "Thieving dragon scum! They pushed us out, left us stranded in the middle of nowhere, and now we have to come here and steal back what's ours."

That was when Rampant made his move.

CHAPTER 17

Out from his shadowy hollow the black dragon sprang.

In a flash he'd snatched Lou up by its woolly skin and, with a flick of his neck, slung the little upright across the flat tops of the wooden lumps, and beyond them into Perilous's dappled chest. Lou let out a frantic yell as it made its short flight and found itself clasped by a dragon; a huge green one who didn't look welcoming at all.

The other uprights, led by Lou's dag, came swarming towards the back of the cave, waving fire-sticks and shouting furiously. Rampant didn't wait for them to reach him. He charged forward, roaring and flashing his claws and breathing flames a full dragon's length ahead of him. It was this that stopped the uprights in their tracks, turned them, and sent them fleeing pell-mell out of the cave.

All but one.

Lou's dag stood his ground, putting his hands up to shield his face against the flames licking towards him, as Rampant stood, roaring between huge gouts of fire, twisting his head ferociously, eyes glaring, tearing at the air with his giant claws.

"Give me my daughter!" the upright shouted. "Do what you like with me, but don't hurt her!"

Her? So, Red thought, Lou must be female!

He'd watched Rampant charge with a mix of pride and startled amazement. He didn't know his dag could be so fierce and furious; he'd seen him breathe fire for practice, but never like this! Red, the hotness behind his eyes now scorching, jumped onto the top of the blocks and shouted too.

"Please, Dag, *please* – CEASE FIRE!"

With a loud snap, Rampant clamped his jaws closed, shutting off the searing outpour. He turned, and Red saw Lou's dag lower his hands.

Lou, struggling in Perilous's paws, shrieked, "Let me go! Let me go! Dad, are you hurt?"

Red's mag – suddenly and shockingly aware that she was frightening such a young one – put Lou down gently on the floor. The moment she did, the little upright scampered around the blocks straight into her dag's waiting embrace. He lifted her in the air and hugged her to his scorched sweater (even now the new word came into Red's think-space).

Then Red heard Lou say, in a muffled, shaky voice, "You didn't run away, Dad!"

"How could I leave you?"

As Red watched Lou and her dag holding each other tightly with their front legs, he couldn't help thinking that uprights weren't just very clever. They were very *brave*, too.

Red's mag came around the wooden lumps in a series of jumps, straight past Rampant and Lou and her dag standing in the middle of the cave, and out into the open inlet.

"Where's Mag going?" asked Red.

Rampant peered after his pair. "Out for some air, I expect, and who can blame her! We've been stuck here for Flame knows how long, hiding like animals."

Red jumped over to the uprights.

"Sorry about my dag," he said politely. The upright full-grown was still breathing heavily, his eyes wide with fear. His sweater, Red could see, wasn't so much scorched as burned through. "It's just … it's hard for him to forget…"

"Forget what?" asked Lou.

"That one of you put a hole in him."

"And while we're talking about things that are hard to forget," barked Rampant, "I'm still struggling with the whole thieving-dragon-scum-pushing-you-out-into-the-middle-of-nowhere business. And while we're also sharing our *feelings*, I don't care to be called names, WHATEVER THEY MEAN!"

Ignoring his dag, Red bent his head till it was level with Lou's and blew a little gentle smoke in her face. It got lost in her hair.

"Are you all right?" he asked.

"My trousers are torn," she replied. Then she added shakily, "Your dad scared me."

"Yes, I'm sorry.""

"The other one – the green one—"

"You mean my mag?"

"Your … yes, that one. She seems … gentler."

"Mag? *Gentle*? You should see her when you haven't done your cave-work—"

"Lou! Come away from those creatures!" Lou's dag ordered, grabbing her tightly by the hand and turning towards the entrance. But Rampant, in an astonishing burst of dragonly speed, got there first. He towered before them, blocking their escape – head lowered, wings spread like a wall, breathing dark warning-smoke and uttering faint, threatening growls.

"You're not going anywhere," he hissed.

CHAPTER 18

Perilous reappeared in the cave mouth panting little pale puffs.

"I've seen them – the other uprights," she said. "They got back into the wet-floater and pushed off."

Lou and her dag looked at each other in horror.

"Is it true? Have the others really left us?" squeaked Lou.

Her dag peered nervously beyond the mouth of the cave towards the Endless Water and caught a glimpse of the other uprights. Sure enough, there they were, clear to see, pulling furiously against the waves. He nodded.

"Cowards," Lou murmured.

"Well, it's hard to be brave when you're scared out of your wits." Lou's *dad* shot the dragons an accusing look.

"You were scared too, Dad. And *you* didn't run away."

He turned to her and put his hands on her shoulders. "It was different for me. You're my child – my one and only. If I lost you—" His voice cracked slightly. "If that happened, I'd have nothing left."

Red had no experience of upright faces, but when their mouths turned down at the corners, he somehow knew it was a bad thing. The big one gave the smaller one a pat.

My dag does that to *me*, Red realized, stunned. Could uprights have feelings too?

Suddenly the idea Red had had – about grabbing an upright – didn't seem so clever after all. Now what? Lou had some water coming out of her eyes. Tiny drops like rain on leaves. The sight made him feel uncomfortable. He glanced at his dag.

"What's the plan?"

In answer, Rampant jumped closer to the two uprights, so close they took a quick step back.

"I brought something," he announced. Then, with a solemn air, he reached his snout down into his pouch and drew out the Block of Knowledge, holding it carefully between his teeth. He laid it on the ground before them.

The uprights exchanged looks but didn't speak.

"Our wise dragons," Rampant explained, "have always had it in their think-spaces that Blocks of Knowledge, like this one, contain secrets."

"Secrets?" echoed Lou's dag warily.

"Yes, but we don't know" – Rampant cleared his throat, finding it difficult to admit – "what they are."

Again the uprights glanced at each other – confused, Red could tell. And suddenly Lou's dag's expression changed.

"You mean," he said, very slowly, "you can't read?"

Now it was the dragons who all looked at one another.

"What is *read*?" asked Rampant.

"Read – *read* – you know, the words in this book… Or block, you said." There was silence. Lou's dag shook his head despairingly. "All right. I'll look." He bent down and reached out to pick it up. But Rampant, on an impulse, lurched forward, letting out a threatening growl. The hand was snapped back.

"Take it easy, big fella! I can't tell you anything if you don't let me pick it up."

"Let him, Dag," Red urged.

Rampant hesitated briefly, then moved back a little. Lou's dag, still a bit shaken, bent down cautiously and picked up the book. He looked at the top of it for a moment. Letting his wormy things play over the marks, he said, *"A Visual Compendium of Wonders From..."* He peered closer. *"Wonders From..."*

Lou's face pressed in beside his. *"Nature!"* she finished excitedly.

The two uprights stared at each other for a moment, wide-eyed with wonder. Then the big one opened it. And his face changed again.

"Incredible..." he whispered. "Like a miracle – perfectly preserved." He looked up at Red's dag, his eyes blazing. "Where in this ruined world did you find it?"

"That doesn't matter," said Rampant sternly. "What matters is what's inside."

There was a pause, while Lou's dag turned the book in his hands, caressing one flat side. Then he looked up again.

"There aren't any secrets. Only written words," he said.

"Written words? What's *that*?" asked Rampant suspiciously.

Lou's dag pointed at the mass of black lines. "These."

The dragons gathered round, looking first at the black lines then at each other.

Suddenly Red's voice exploded. "Those marks! They're words – don't you see? – they are WORDS!" He turned to his mag and dag and said gleefully, "All this time -- *words*!"

"Are you saying you didn't *know* that?" asked Lou, astonished.

Red shook his head vigorously. "Well, no one ever said!"

Lou's dag straightened; his tone changed. "When you took our books, you took our history – our stories, our beginnings and our endings. You took *all* of it … and guess what? You can't even read them!"

For a moment, there was silence, then: "*Books?*" Red said suddenly. "Is – is *that* your word for our Blocks of Knowledge?"

Lou's dag turned and looked at the red dragon.

"That's right," he said quietly. "Through all of it – the madness and the greed and the ruin – we still had books. They were the one good thing. We filled them with imagination and stories and wisdom. Dragons aren't the only clever ones. We had some clever people too, you know, before…" He cleared his throat. "Books are all that's left of them. If you can't read them – if you can't do *that* – then you might as well bury the lot."

❧

"Are you saying books can talk?" Red gasped. His think-space had become a fireball of excited curiosity.

"Well – yes, in a way," said Lou's dag. "This one, the *Compendium*, talks about animals mostly. And it shows them – in pictures."

The dragons didn't say anything; they just stared vaguely at the book.

Lou nudged her dag. "They don't know what

pictures are, Dad," she whispered. "You'll have to show them."

"*You* show them," he said, and handed her the book. She held it, resting it on one front leg, and stroked it as if it were something beloved. Then, very slowly and delicately, she opened it.

Red edged closer.

"Look," she said. "Isn't this wonderful?"

Red peered over her shoulder. "Yes..."

"You want me to read some of it?"

"*Read?*"

"Yes, you know – make the book talk."

"Oh, yes please," said Red eagerly.

Behind him Rampant and Perilous shuffled uncomfortably. Lou put one of her wormy things on a leaf and moved it along one of the black lines, and said, "Polar bears used ice for travelling, food, shelter, mating and dens. As their homes began to disappear because of a change in climate—"

"*Cli-maaate,*" repeated Red, without thinking.

"That's right." She went on. "They were listed as a threatened species. With the disappearance of their homes, they spent more time on land, and, despite the dire warnings, became extinct in..."

Lou stopped reading. She and her dag exchanged looks.

"Right, then," said her dag, giving a nervous little cough, "that's enough book-talking for today."

There was silence.

"I just had a think," said Red. "The *pic-tur* things – they're like the ones we saw in the town-place."

"Town-place?" said Lou's dag, suddenly interested. "Hang on – you mean you've seen a *town*?" He jumped to his feet, startling Red. "Where? Where was it? Tell me – were there any people there?"

Rampant pushed forward threateningly. "Careful, upright," he warned.

Lou knew Red wouldn't know this word. "Us," she explained. "*We're* people."

"You mean uprights!"

Rampant drew himself to his full height. "Of course there weren't any uprights," he growled. "How could there be? There haven't been any on the mainland since the Great Ridding."

"That's right. Of course not," said Lou's dag. "Not since *you* lot drove us away."

A cold silence fell in the cave.

"We had no choice." Rampant stared at Lou's dag,

and Lou's dag stared right back. The air was suddenly crackling with danger. Rampant grunted, and brown warning-smoke trailed from his nostrils.

"You stole our live-spaces," Rampant said. "You spoiled the air and the water. We rid ourselves of uprights because you didn't deserve to live here any more. If we'd let you stay, there wouldn't *be* a mainland – there wouldn't be *anything* left at all!"

Their faces were now no more than a dragon's tongue apart, Rampant's nostrils flaring, back-fins bristling, and he was hot behind the eyes – hotter than ever before. He felt something, from far back along the Trail, and he knew it was terrible and wrong and deadly. And yet welcome, all at once. The feeling started as a hot tingling in his chest, and then quickly rose in him – higher and higher until it felt like it would burst out in flames—

"Please, Dag." Red was tugging on his paw. Then he added in a timid voice, "Be *decent*."

That one word, and the sight of his mumbo gazing up at him with beseeching eyes, calmed the black dragon, turning his dark smoke white again. He retreated. As soon as he did the full-grown upright let out his tightly held breath in relief.

Red's attention returned to the book. He pointed to a strange animal with his tail-point. "What's that?"

Lou peered at it. "I think it's a tiger."

"*Ti-ger,*" repeated Red, running the word around his mouth as if he were tasting some delicious morsel.

"They're all gone now. Like the polar bear."

"Gone? Where did they go?"

"They're dead, Red; they're all dead."

She could see the small dragon didn't understand so she made a strange face, closing her eyes, pulling the corners of her mouth down, and sticking her tongue out.

Red looked at her quizzically. "You mean ... life-over?"

"Yes. Now we've only got these..."

"Pic-turs," said Red slowly. He turned to his mag and dag. "Those things we saw in the town-place – the look-likes – maybe they were pic-turs too. There were lots of them, all in one built-thing."

"There must've been an art gallery left standing in that ... town-place," said Lou excitedly. "Oh! If only I could see it – not just in books, but here in the world, in *real life*!" She looked at Red, and the other two dragons behind him. "Do dragons know about art?" she asked.

Red said, sadly, "Is art pic-turs? Don't you need hands for causing that?"

"No. You can do art with anything – hands, feet, even your teeth. But it all starts here" – she tapped the side of her head – "in your imagination."

Red felt something burst inside his think-space. Like when the first rays of the light-shine come up and chase away the dark. He suddenly wanted to pick Lou up and carry her away to some place where no full-grown could interrupt, and ask her for more new words … words for the most wonderful, extraordinary, fascinating things.

Imagination.

It had the sound of beautiful newness. Like the start of warm-time when everything is bursting, and anything is possible.

CHAPTER 19

The two uprights, abandoned by their friends, left for dead in a cave and kept hostage by three dragons – two of which had made it clear they would tear them to pieces or burn them to a crisp if they didn't do exactly as they were told – were finding it difficult not to feel incredibly afraid. Every time one of the dragons moved, Lou and her dag felt a little leap in their chests, though they tried very hard not to show it.

Rampant, who'd been looking at the book, using his tongue very delicately to turn the leaves, suddenly exclaimed, "Look! There are dragons here – in the pic-turs."

Lou was almost too afraid to look. After all, she'd only just read about what humans had done to the world, letting creatures go extinct.

She answered cautiously. "Perhaps … perhaps someone studied them – long ago – and wrote about them and made pictures."

Rampant turned another leaf. "It's strange," he whispered to his pair. "Uprights *learning* about us. Why would they do that? They *hated* us."

"And we hated them, too. We still do."

"Maybe whoever caused the block – I mean, book – *didn't* hate us," reasoned Red. "Maybe they *liked* us."

His dag stared at him. Rampant shook his head. "Think about the stone upright – the one we saw in the town-place, sticking that pointed thing into the dragon." Red nodded. "They *couldn't* have liked us."

Lou looked at the black dragon curiously. "Did you say *sticking*?" she asked. "You mean – trying to kill?" Rampant nodded. "I think that might be Saint George and the dragon."

"Who?"

There was something about the way Red asked, and the way his dag seemed to rise in response, that made Lou stop talking.

"Look," said Lou's dag, trying to break the tension, "you know it's not real, the whole Saint George and the dragon thing. It was all made up…"

"Made *up*?"

"Yeah. It's a story, just a silly story."

"I like stories," said Red. "I cause behind-the-eyes

stories all the time." Then he added coolly, "Just not ones where peepuls stick things into dragons."

Red's mag hadn't been listening to this conversation. She had been too busy sampling the bits of cooked food scattered around the burned-out fire. Now she lifted her head.

"Ferocity. Bring that young upright over here, will you?"

Leaving the two full-growns with the book, Red lowered his head, and, with his horns, gently butted Lou in the back.

"Hey! Stop pushing!" she complained but moved where he nudged her until she was standing in front of Perilous.

The green dragon gazed at her for a moment, then asked in her very best white-smoke voice, "Tell me your name again?"

"Lou. What's yours?"

The idea of an upright, especially one so young, asking her – a dragon – such an up-close question seemed rude. Perilous gave a little affronted snort before answering, "Perilous Bychaheadoff."

Lou's dag looked up, startled. Lou clapped her hand to her mouth.

"It's a very popular dragon name," Perilous said. "As for yours, it's rather short, isn't it? Isn't there more to it?"

"You mean our *last* name? Well, yes, it's—" But Lou stopped suddenly, and her face flushed almost as red as Red's.

"Go ahead, you might as well tell them," her dag muttered.

Lou hesitated then said, in a small voice, "Killdragon."

All three dragons stiffened.

"Kill … *dragon*? But that's a horrible name!" exclaimed Perilous.

"Oh? And I suppose *bite your head off* is what, exactly? Friendly?"

"Bychaheadoff happens to be a very old, very *decent* dragon's name," said Rampant confidently.

"And it doesn't actually mean that we bite uprights' heads off or anything," Red assured her.

"Well, actually we *did*. When we had to!" growled Rampant.

"You should be ashamed to even say it," snapped Lou's dag, "considering you drove us off our land!"

Perilous drew herself up to her full height so that Lou's dag – Killdragon – had to tilt his head right back to gaze up at her.

"Your land, as you *dare* to call it," she said haughtily, "belonged to *all* of us. Every single living creature. But your share was never enough for you. You had to have it all!"

Killdragon scoffed. "What about *your* ancestors?"

"What about them?" Rampant snarled.

"A bunch of dumb, fire-breathing man-eaters! Constantly attacking us and standing in the way of progress!"

Rampant's nostrils started to stream dark smoke. "Progress," he growled. "PROGRESS! Is that what you *dare* call it? Tell me, is it progress to ruin everything you touch?"

"Whatever we touched made the world hotter," said Killdragon. "And your kind *loved* it that way! All that so-called *ruining* we 'uprights' did wound up making you lot cleverer. Come to think of it, instead of standing there growling, you should probably just thank us and be on your way!"

That did it.

Perilous thrust her head forward and opened her jaws wide, as if she were about to live up to her name, when—

"NOOOO!" shouted Red.

His mag froze. Her more decent and civilized dragonly part took hold and shook the rage out of her. She withdrew, closing her mouth.

There was a shocked silence.

They all knew something terrible had very nearly happened. Perilous felt her son put a paw on her neck.

"Thank you," he said quietly, and slowly her smoke paled.

"All right," his mag said firmly. "Let's all settle down. And be decent."

Then Red said something he'd heard in school. Suddenly it wasn't just words; it really meant something.

"Dragon tail and dragon wing, find what decency may bring. Dragon tooth and dragon fin, fights are things no one can win—"

His mag and dag joined in, their voices booming in the cave:

"DRAGON SCALE AND DRAGON CLAW, TALK, DON'T QUARREL ANY MORE!"

With their think-spaces clearer, and their smoke a reassuring pale grey, the dragons promptly crouched around the dwindling fire, leaving space for the uprights to close the circle. Lou and her dag exchanged relieved glances, then Killdragon turned to the others.

"All right," he said. "Let's talk. Man to dragon."

"Dragon to man," corrected Rampant.

And so they began.

The dragons and the uprights had a long heads-together, during which a lot of accusations were made about the Old Time. It became clear that each side wanted something from the other, but after so long as enemies, neither wanted to be first to ask. Until finally Rampant came out with it.

"We've caught you now. You have to do what we want."

"And what's that, then?" asked Killdragon suspiciously.

"Come back with us – to our live-place – to help us."

"Help you? How?"

The full-grown dragons exchanged looks. This wasn't going to be easy to admit. They could make themselves vulnerable.

"We need coal … er … for our chest-fires."

"Coal?"

"We eat it."

"You *eat* it?"

"Yes. And our stocks have almost run out."

"So?"

"If we can't get coal" – Rampant hesitated, clearing his throat – "if we can't get coal…"

"Yes?"

"We just need it, that's all," put in Perilous, before her pair could give too much away. "And we want you to show us how to get it."

"We have coal," said Lou, "back home – on our island."

A stunned silence fell in the cave.

"You have *coal*?" said Rampant, his voice reduced to an enthralled whisper.

The two uprights exchanged glances.

"Er, yes, we have it," said Killdragon. "But we're not just going to *give* it away. What do we get for it?"

"What do you want?" asked Perilous.

"I'll tell you. We want to be able to come here – to the mainland – and collect supplies: tins of food, tools, machines, things our kind left behind. Things we can't grow or make on the island. We need access – to be able to come here safely."

There was a pause.

"We can't come back with you," Lou said.

They all looked at her.

"Why not?" asked Red.

"It's much too far. And you can't carry us."

"Of course we can – in our teeth!" said Rampant.

Killdragon jumped up. "If you think I'm going to let you carry my daughter in your jaws like some dead thing," he shouted, "you've got another think coming, dragon!"

"We should take *them* back with *us* – to our island," said Lou.

"No. We're not flying over the Endless Water," said Perilous, bristling. "Not with my son."

"We'll take you on the cat."

Lou's dad looked at her, shocked. "Our boat?" he asked. "You must be joking!"

"I'm not going on that wet-floater!" roared Rampant.

"It's better than flying," reasoned Red.

"We need a family heads-together," said Perilous sharply. "Outside."

The dragons jumped out of the cave, far enough so the uprights couldn't hear them. They huddled on the edge of the water with their wings unfolded to make a little private enclosure.

"I don't like it," said Rampant. "We don't know how far it is and we'll be stuck on that wet-floater out there with uprights! They'll try to end us. And what if that little she-upright's lying about coal – what then? Once we get to their land-lump there'll be *more* of them. And another thing. How will we get home?"

"How indeed?" agreed Perilous.

"I don't think she's lying, Dag, I really don't."

"How do you know?"

"I can feel it in my think-space."

"Oh, shut up about your flaming think-space!" growled his dag.

When they returned to cave, Killdragon was holding some strange objects. He must have taken them out of the blocks because, Red noticed, one had been opened.

Rampant, the moment he saw them, drew back and snarled, "What've you got in your hands?"

"Flares – they're just flares. They were in one of the crates."

Killdragon showed him. They looked like broken-off branches.

"What are *flares*?"

"They're something we use for signalling."

"Signalling?" said Red, excitedly. "*We* do that too – with smoke or our tails."

"We use these," said Killdragon.

Red stood there staring at the flares and realized, with growing unease, that signalling was something else that dragons and uprights had in common.

BLOCK VI
JOURNEY TO
UPRIGHT ISLAND

CHAPTER 20

Flares turned out to be one of the most exciting things Red had ever seen. Lou stuck one into the sand by the water, and her dag, after telling them to stand back, lit the end with a tiny piece of glowing wood. There was a hissing sound and then—

WHOOOSH! Something went shooting up into the sky and burst in a shower of bright falling sky-sparks.

"You can trap fire in those little tree pieces?" Perilous said, amazed.

"Can I light the next one?" asked Red, thrilled.

Somehow the excitement of this task made him able to produce a very small but adequate flame to light the other flare. Up it went like the first. Rampant was too excited by Red's first ever flame to notice.

"You did it, son! You *finally* did it!"

"Told you..." Perilous said under her breath.

Red felt a rush of pride. He was a proper half-grown now!

Lou's dag let out a short sigh of relief. "I was afraid they might have got damp in that cave. Lucky they were well wrapped."

Perilous set about exploring the *wrappings*. They were made of some stuff she'd never seen before. This too was a source of awe.

She muttered into her pair's ear, "You can't say they're not clever, Rampant. Not after that."

Rampant grunted dismissively. "What puzzles me is how anything can be so clever and so *stupid* at the same time!"

The flares, bright as they were, didn't seem to have any effect. The two uprights waited on the shore, staring hopefully out at the wet-floater. Red, whose eyesight was better than his parents', could see the uprights still there, and guessed that the signal was meant to bring them back.

Red turned to Lou and asked, "Who are they, those other peepuls out there?"

"They're villagers from our island."

"*Vill-a-jar?*"

"Some are sailors; they're the ones that make

the big boat go through the water. The others are searchers; they come ashore and look for the things we need."

"Bad-doers, you mean?"

Lou looked at him. "What's a bad-doer?"

"Someone who does something wrong."

"They're only trying to survive," she said, defensively. "If that makes them wrong-doers, then your kind are wrong-doers too." Red didn't say anything. "Anyway, what else can we do? After we were driven off the mainland, a lot of us died—"

"You mean life-over?"

She nodded solemnly. "There wasn't enough food or shelter on the islands. There was a lot of fighting and people killing each other. The ones that survived built shelters, grew crops – some even managed to raise animals for wool. But our numbers grew; and in the end, there wasn't enough to go round."

"So *that's* why you come to the mainland."

"We have no choice."

That made Red feel better. Having no choice was something he knew all about. Having no choice meant doing whatever needed to be done. Even his dag had said that sometimes laws had to be broken.

As the light-shine began to fade, so did Perilous's resolve. She turned to her pair and whispered, "I wanted to show them dragons are better. I wanted to prove them wrong about us. But I'm hungry and cold, and I'm worried sick about Ferocity." She glanced over at her son, crouched next to Lou by the water's edge. Perilous lowered her voice further. "The uprights seem to be winning him over."

The thought of that hurt Rampant much worse than when they'd made a hole in his scale.

"All right, enough waiting!" he growled. "If we're going, let's go!" He shook his wings as if to test the wind, then turned to Killdragon, who was staring out across the water. "Your mumbo can ride on the back of ours," said Rampant. "His fins are still soft enough for her to flatten. I'll carry *you* in my paws—"

Killdragon spun round. *"Your paws?"*

"Yes. Unless of course" – the black dragon's voice took on a menacing tone – "you'd prefer it if I picked you up *in my teeth?*"

Lou was grimacing. "Are those things on your back your fins?" she asked Red. "Because there's no way I'm sitting on those."

Red turned his back to her. "You have to push them

down," he explained. "Press them flat – all one way."

He felt her warm hands on two of the sharp sticking-out fins that went all the way down his spine. She pressed them to one side. The moment she let go, they sprang back up again.

"You'll have to sit on me to keep them down," he said, and he crouched as low as he could, while the full-growns – dragons and upright – looked on.

Lou scrambled up, using Red's thick tail and haunch as steps. Then she pushed the two fins down and straddled him between two more, gripping his sides with her knees.

"Ow! The next spike's sticking into my chest!" she complained.

"Push it down and lean against me to hold it flat."

Red's mag and dag were still staring and feeling decidedly uncomfortable.

"I never thought I'd live to see the light," murmured Perilous. "A *dragon* carrying an *upright*—"

"It's just not *decent*," muttered Rampant. He and Killdragon locked eyes. Neither knew what was in the other's think-space.

"Don't – squeeze – my – *throat*!" Red croaked.

Lou took her arm from around his neck and tried

to relax, but her initial enthusiasm was fast being overtaken by the horrifying reality: Red was about to take off!

"I'm scared I might fall," she whispered.

"Don't be," he said. "Hold on tight with your front legs, and you'll be safe."

Perilous jumped closer. "Are you sure she's not too heavy for you, Ferocity?"

"Don't worry, Mag!"

Never having carried anything heavier than a fur-hopper in his jaws, and never anything on his back, Red really wasn't sure he could manage, especially over water. In the last few moments before take-off, he felt a surge of unease. But it would take more than *that* to stop him!

Rampant jumped over to Killdragon and asked him to slip the block back into his pouch. Then he picked him up under the arms.

"Ow! That hurts!" yelled the upright, his long back legs dangling down.

"Are you sure your dad can carry him?" Lou whispered doubtfully.

"Course I'm sure," said Red confidently, as if his family made a habit of carrying uprights across the Endless Water.

Moments later, Rampant was jumping along the shore, trying frantically to make his wings lift him and his flailing passenger into the air. Finally he managed to get airborne – *just* – and swung bravely out over the water.

Killdragon, feet trailing through the surf, shouted, "Higher – FLY HIGHER!"

Rampant, heaving gouts of smoke and tearing at the air with his wings, flapped furiously, but he just couldn't rise above the waves. He knew he'd never make it to the wet-floater, and that the more he tried now the less likely it was, if he failed, he'd find the strength to make it back to shore. He turned and went back.

After a brief recovery time, he tried again – and *again* – until he felt his wing muscles ache as never before, while the burdensome upright clung on tight and bounced every time his carrier-dragon came down to earth.

"This isn't working," groaned Killdragon.

Lou, who'd turned a neat somersault after her

carrier-dragon had made several equally fruitless attempts at take-off, picked herself up and brushed the sand out of her hair.

"What about trying up there?" she asked, pointing at the clifftop.

The dragons all looked at her aghast.

"I couldn't fly up there now," Rampant gasped, "even *without* carrying anything. I'm exhausted!"

"Then we'll have to climb," said Killdragon.

"*Climb?*"

"We do it all the time when we come for—"
The upright stopped abruptly.

Rampant narrowed his eyes. "You mean when you're sneaking around?"

"*Trying* to survive."

"By taking things from us – from dragonland?" Rampant's voice had taken on its threatening tone again.

"So what? You think we *enjoy* coming here – to constant danger – scavenging for the things our ancestors left behind? You think we need reminding that you drove them away? Well, we don't. We do what we have to do to *survive*," said Killdragon furiously.

What followed was another aching silence when the

trials of generations seemed to rush to the surface like boiling hot geysers, ready to erupt. Just before they did, Perilous stepped forward.

"Show us," she said quietly. "Please."

Killdragon led them to the far end of the inlet, where the sand-flapper pools were. There the dragons saw, for the first time, that there were steps cut into the cliff face, quite steep and winding out of sight in the folds of the precipice.

"What d'you take us for – horn-trotters?" Rampant grumbled. "We can't get up there!"

"Come on, Dag!" prompted Red, jumping forward and gazing up at the cliff face undaunted. "We can do it."

"Dragons don't do cliffs," his dag mumbled. But it was no use.

Lou and her dag climbed the dangerous steps in the dark, feeling their way. Luckily the dark-shine had risen now, and the uprights had done it before, so their feet and hands knew the steps well.

For the dragons it was much harder. Their big back feet found little room on the steps for jumping, and they had to hold on with their front claws and use their

tails to stop themselves
from falling backwards.
Puffing with effort,
the five of them finally
gathered at the top.

The dark-shine had
sailed serenely through
the clouds, lighting the
Endless Water with its
mysterious and beautiful
glow, revealing the big
wet-floater bobbing up
and down a long way
from shore.

"Look!" Lou cried.
"See those lamps, fore
and aft? That'll give us
our target."

Lam-pss, thought Red.
Another wonderful new
word!

Killdragon turned to
Rampant. "What if I'm
too heavy for you?"

"I have a plan," Perilous said proudly. "Rampant and I will carry you between us."

"How?" asked Killdragon in alarm.

"I'll wrap my tail around you and take off. Rampant will fly underneath." Her pair gave her a disbelieving look, but Perilous continued, "You'll stand on him, and he'll take most of your weight on his shoulders."

Was it the dark-shine light or had Killdragon turned green?

"And I'll ride on Red!" Lou said. She put her front leg around his neck trustingly. "We call this a hug," she whispered.

"I know," he whispered back. "Dragons do hugs too."

Tails are not meant for lifting things. The moment Perilous and her upright passenger were off the cliff, the weight pulled her tail straight down, and her with it. No matter how hard she beat her wings, she couldn't prevent herself from sinking. Watching them from the clifftop, Red's smoke stopped in his chest. But at the last moment—

WHOOOSH! His dag swooped under them and

thrust his massive shoulders up against Killdragon's dangling feet, taking most of the weight.

"That's it! That's it!" yelled Killdragon excitedly. "WE'RE GOING TO MAKE IT!"

They flew higher, and now they were out over the water, with the dark-shine light on their backs and Lou's dag, as upright as an upright could be, between them. Lou, like Red, was watching, waving her front legs as if they were wings, and dancing up and down.

"Come on, Red, or we'll be left behind!" she cried, as the flapping noise of the full-growns' great wings grew fainter.

Red crouched and Lou climbed onto his back, pushing down his fins as before. He shuffled to the brink and stood there, his back claws just curling over the edge, and took a deep breath.

Then he froze, unable to move.

There ought, he reckoned, to be something you could do now – some trick that would make the impossible possible. Suddenly, as if in answer to his think, Lou shouted, *"ANGELS AND MINISTERS OF GRACE DEFEND US!"* at the top of her voice.

The words rang out across the shimmering expanse far below. And though Red hadn't the faintest think what they meant, they seemed to fill him to the knobbly tips of his horns with reckless courage. His wings spread by themselves and next thing he knew …

… he was leaping off the cliff!

With a sudden rushing dip that brought him, for a heart-stop, only a flame's length from a tail-wetting, he was flying straight out over the Endless Water, with Lou clinging on for dear life. She tried to croak out again, *"Angels and ministers…"*

But the magic words blew away on the onrush of wind.

CHAPTER 21

Landing between two lights on the big wet-floater was the hardest piece of flying Rampant had ever done. It didn't help that the wet-floater turned out to be *two* floaters joined in the middle by a flat part, and with a big wing flapping over it all, making it hard to see.

Rampant did the only thing possible. He let himself drop, aiming for the flat part, but he missed it and came down instead on one of the small floaters. The other floater lifted, tilting Rampant's end, nearly pitching him, Perilous and Killdragon into the water.

Red, above and behind them, saw this happen and panicked, fearing his parents would fall in – which they very nearly did. Meanwhile, Killdragon was yelling at Perilous, still airborne above him, "Throw yourself across to the lifted part and press it back down!"

By the time she'd managed to do this – dragging Lou's dag still entangled in her tail behind her – there

185

was uproar on the wet-floater. Several uprights seemed to have burst out of nowhere and were swarming all over it in the dark, making loud noises. Even by dark-shine light it was clear to Red that what his dag had warned might happen was right: the uprights wanted to push the dragons off the wet-floater!

And if it hadn't been for Lou, they might have done it, too.

The full-growns were so confused by all the noise and by the violent rocking of the floaters that they almost fell in by themselves. But as Red came sailing down, Lou started shouting to the uprights below. They all stopped and stared upward, the dark-shine light reflecting off their frightened faces.

"Look at me! Look! I'm riding a dragon!" Lou yelled.

She was obviously unharmed, even happy, and all the uprights could do was gape and goggle. The wet-floater had been righted – a full-grown dragon perched on each half – by the time Red made a crash-landing onto the flat bit in the middle. Lou, laughing triumphantly, fell off, almost on top of her dag, who was struggling to unwrap Perilous's tail from around his waist.

"It's all right!" Killdragon shouted to the others.

"They're with us! They brought us back. Don't hurt them!"

"Don't hurt them? Don't hurt *them*! Oh, that's good; I like *that*!" snorted Rampant.

And now there were so many other voices shouting that it was hard to make the words out, but they were saying things like, "Get those things off the ship!" and "Kill them – kill them ALL!"

"Good dragon-light to you, too," muttered Rampant sarcastically under his dark smoky breath.

By the time the wet-floater – or *catamaran*, as Lou called it – started its journey, the uprights were subdued. They kept sneaking sideways glances at the dragons, obviously terrified of them and not knowing what to make of this appalling situation.

"Killdragon must've talked some dragonsense into them," whispered Perilous to her pair.

"How d'you know?"

"Because they haven't tried to stick us with anything yet."

Red hadn't noticed the strange looks. He was too excited watching the peepuls running about doing things to the – what was Lou's other word? – *boat* to make it go, and getting in the way, poking his snout into everything. And asking endless questions.

He particularly liked the tall, branchless tree that held the big, billowing wing that caught the wind and pulled the boat across the water. Red understood this because the wind could do the same to his wings. He soon found out from Lou that this thing was called a *sail* and the tree was a *mast*. He was learning new words with every flick of his ears – and loving it!

But soon Killdragon came and asked him to please leave the peepuls alone to get on with their work. After that, Red just scrambled back and forth across the middle of the boat, between his parents, who had to crouch separately on the floating parts on each side to keep it from tilting. They were both nervous and jumpy.

When next light came, Red found himself peering back towards the mainland, watching it get smaller and smaller. Then it finally vanished – the way the light-shine did at dark – and he felt a strange ache inside. It was as if part of him had disappeared with it.

And he wondered if he would ever get that part back.

CHAPTER 22

The voyage was long and rough, and if Perilous's skin hadn't already been green, that's the colour it would have turned from all the up and downing on the wet-floater. Rampant managed to take his think-space off the endless rocking by catching sand-flappers, some of which obligingly leaped right out of the water into his gaping jaws. These kept the dragon family's hunger at bay.

But thirst was still a problem. When Red tried to take a drink of seawater, Killdragon grabbed him and pulled him back.

"NO!" he cried. "Don't drink that stuff; it'll drive you crazy."

"*Cray-zeee?*"

"Yes, you know – in the head!" He tapped the side of his head vigorously.

"Life-over?" sputtered Red.

"Worse."

There was a supply of fresh water in round wooden things – *barrels* – which Lou told Red was the only kind they should drink. But there wasn't much of it, and the rest of the uprights tried to keep it to themselves, even after several lights and darks. They were now treating their dragon passengers with unmistakable hostility. The little red one was mostly just a nuisance, but the two big ones seemed to be angry most of the time, growling and puffing dark smoke.

The uprights avoided them.

That tactic seemed to work until one dark, Perilous, whose creeping thirst had finally pushed her to the brink, shot a quick blast of fire at some uprights who were using sticks to prod and poke Red away from the water barrels. The supply became more available after that, but they still made faces at him when he passed, which – because he understood their meaning now – made him uncomfortable.

Soon after that, and luckily for all on board, it rained.

Red watched the uprights stand about, their heads tilted back, their jaws open wide to the sky, with their funny-looking tongues sticking out. They used more barrels to trap as much falling water as they could.

Red marvelled. He could tell, of course, that his mag and dag were hating every floater-lifting and floater-dropping moment, and he certainly didn't want to admit to them what a smoke-stopping adventure *he* was having, despite the hardships. Or how thrilled he was to be going to Upright Island for fear it might seem disloyal to dragonkind.

There was no land to be seen, just water stretching out in every direction, and for dragons who'd never gone much further than their own small live-space, there was something extremely discomforting about its cavelessness. And always the dread of falling in!

Lou gave a long recite about it that began: "*Water, water, everywhere, nor any drop to drink…*"

Red liked this a lot and told her she had a wonderful think-space to cause such beautiful words, but she said it wasn't from her think-space (she called it her *brain*) but from a book.

"Have you got lots of books?"

"A few," she said woefully, "but they're very old and falling to bits. Some of us have tried to learn the words in them by heart but it's hard."

One of the uprights in the cave had said they'd come to the mainland to find books. Now Red understood. Words had to be put into think-spaces to keep them. Red knew he couldn't do that. The little recites they learned at school were nothing compared with what Lou could do.

There were plenty of sand-flappers near the surface that seemed ready to be caught, but sometimes it was a dangerous business. Once, a large one rose alongside one of the side floats and leaped clear, twisting and coming down with a great splash when Rampant

snapped his jaws at it, making the wet-floater tilt dangerously and the uprights yell at him, but it was worth it for the good feast the dragons enjoyed. But even that didn't cheer the black dragon up for long. He had the distinct feeling that his firebox might heave itself right out his mouth when the water went up and down.

They allowed themselves very little coal, small pieces only. Their pouches were nearly empty by now, and as his firebox grew cooler, Rampant felt his strength ebbing away, making him more anxious. If the uprights on the land-lump attacked, would he be able to defend his family?

Perilous crouched on the other floating part and held on tight with her tail wrapped around it. After one particularly large wave lifted the wet-floater up and dropped it down again, Rampant, who'd bounced high in the air and had to spread his wings in order not to fall off, did the same.

Red and Lou sat on the flat part between the two. Except in rough weather, it felt safe and steady in the middle of the boat. They talked over the sound of the *sea* – another new word.

"What d'you think the peepuls on your land-lump will do when they see us?" Red asked.

"They'll probably fall down dead of fright!"

Red reached his snout into his pouch, drew out a bit of coal and crunched it up. "Have any of them ever seen a dragon before?"

"Only in pictures. And there are stories, of course."

Red's ears pricked up. "You have *stories* about us? What kind?"

"Scary ones, mostly."

"We're not scary."

"Your dad was – *really* scary – when he breathed fire at us."

"Only because he thought you were trying to hurt him!" Red said defensively. There was an awkward silence. "They'll hate us," he murmured under smoky breath as the coal caught fire in his chest.

Lou, who'd been lying on her back in the sun, playing idly with Red's tail-point, testing its sharpness on her *finger* (she'd told him what the uprights called their wormy things), sat up sharply.

"They won't hate you. Not once they get to know you. You're too much like us to hate."

Red jerked his head up. "Like *you*?"

"Not to *look* at. I mean inside. Inside, you just want what we want."

"Which is?"

"To survive." She glanced up at the perfect blue dome over their heads and smiled. "And to be happy."

"No more wars?" asked Red hopefully.

"No more wars." Lou spun her body around so she was looking straight at him. "I like you, Red. You're different from everything I thought a dragon would be."

"And what was that?"

"Terrible, ferocious … deadly."

"You're different too."

"What did you think uprights would be like?"

"Terrible, ferocious, deadly."

They looked at each other. Then Lou threw back her head and made a funny cackling.

"What's that noise called?"

"*Laughter* – I'm *laughing*."

Red suddenly felt good inside. "It's like that singing thing you did before – about the Red Dragon."

"We learn that when we're little. It's not just a song; we really believe in him. We believe when he comes, everything bad in the world will go away." After a moment, she said, "Are there a lot of red dragons where you come from?"

"I've never seen one."

Lou gave Red a look of awe.

"Then," she said, swallowing hard, "the song must be about *you*."

CHAPTER 23

Lou's voice took on a more serious tone as she said to Red, "You saved me, you know that? You really did. The others – and I've known most of them since I was little – didn't lift a finger. Not even my cousins. One look at your parents and they fled to the boat! You saw: they were too scared to come back."

"I'd have come back."

"Would you really?"

"Of course. Dragons are decent like that. We always come back."

Lou thought for a moment, gazing out over the gentle waves. Then she looked at Red. "You know what," she said, "I wish I could do something for you."

"You already have. Remember when we were on the cliff, and I couldn't take off? Don't tell my mag and dag, but I was scared. You said something then – some words. I didn't understand most of them, but somehow … somehow they helped me." He paused. "I didn't save you, Lou; your *words* did. Can you teach them to me?"

Lou frowned briefly, then her face lit up. "Oh, you mean, 'Angels and ministers of grace'."

"Yes! That's it. 'Anj-els and min-is-turs of race—'"

"Not *race*!" She laughed. "*Grace*. I say those words to make me brave. And they're not *my* words; they're Shakespeare's."

"*Shake-ssss-pear?*"

"It's the name of a man – I mean an upright – who lived long ago, ages and ages. Long before everything went wrong. He was a writer."

"*Riiii-teeeer…* Uprighter!"

"Oh, Red, you're funny." Lou leaned forward. "Shakespeare wrote lots of wonderful stories. They were called *plays*. I love them because they take me to places that I can never really go."

"You mean in your think-space? Behind-the-eyes stories?"

Lou looked at him curiously. "Yes. In my mind – in my *imagination*."

That word again. Red was pretty sure it was his favourite.

199

"I've learned bits," she continued. "*Passages*, they call them – and I say them to myself sometimes, or out loud when I need to. Like when we were up on that cliff."

She put her arm – their word for front legs – around Red's neck, the dark green sea around them, the sail and the bright sky over their heads.

"Can you tell me some more Shake-spear words?" asked Red.

There was a slight pause while Lou thought, then she said, "*I have been studying how I may compare this prison where I live unto the world…*"

"Slower, speak slower."

200

"I do that a lot," she said wistfully. "Compare my island – which is like a prison – to the mainland and all the wonderful places I can't go."

"What's *pri-zun*?"

"It's somewhere you can't get out of."

"Is that ... is that because we're stopping you?" Red's good feeling vanished.

"There are plenty of things stopping us, not just dragons."

Their conversation was suddenly broken into by a voice: one of the uprights yelling. Lou stood up, her feet wide apart so she could keep her balance on the swaying wet-floater. Using her hand to shield her eyes, she stared out across the sea.

"What is it?" asked Red, getting to his feet. "What's wrong?"

"Nothing," she said, her mouth stretched from one side of her face to the other. "Nothing's wrong. Everything's right." She turned and looked at him, eyes wide. "See, Red? See what's out there?" She turned and pointed, and now he could see it: a dark mass looming on the horizon.

"It's land! Our island. We're nearly home!"

BLOCK VII
THE
ARRIVAL

CHAPTER 24

"It's probably best that you don't show yourselves," Killdragon said. "Not yet, anyway. I'll go first, talk to the elders, let them know you're here, and tell them there's nothing to worry about."

"There *will* be," whispered Rampant, "if they try putting holes in any of us."

But he allowed himself to be led to the middle of the boat and for the sail to be pulled down to hide them from view. Red quickly found a little hole to peep through, and so did the full-growns. None of them could wait to see how the uprights lived.

Dragons don't think ahead much, but Red had tried, during the voyage, to make behind-the-eyes stories of what the land-lump – Lou's *island* – would be like. He'd filled his think-space with pic-turs of a town-place, only not ruined like the one they'd seen, but new and clever and full of wonderful built-things and exciting trappings – another sort of world where the Power of the Hand would show itself in ways he couldn't begin to *imagine*. And there'd be strange creatures – like the tiger and the polar bear in the book – entirely different from the peaceful kind that meat-feeding dragons ended for food.

But when the boat drew close to shore, the dragons, peering through the sail-holes, saw not a big, exciting town but a sad-looking place, with clusters of things that didn't look like proper upright built-things at all. They were made not of strong hard stuff that could stand up high, but of wood covered with leaves and dried grass. There were walls made of branches, with living things in them, and they certainly weren't *tigers*. Ground-flappers scampered about, like the ones back home.

Most of the land the dragons observed was covered with growing stuff in blocks: a pale yellow patch here, a dark green one there. Behind were woods, and behind those, hills. Strangest of all was how many straight lines there were. *Straight*, Red had come to learn, was an upright thing. Nothing looked as if it had just happened. Everything looked Power-of-the-Hand-caused. But it should have been more impressive.

"So *this* is how uprights do things, is it?" Rampant mumbled. "Give me cave any day!"

"It's good there's a hill," said his pair. "It'll help if we have to make a quick escape."

Escape? That wouldn't have occurred to Red. Because how could they? There was no way they could fly back – not to where the wet-floater had taken them from. Well, no use worrying about it now. He was too busy hoping he wasn't going to be disappointed, that he'd be able to say nice things to Lou about her home.

"Perhaps we're only seeing the edge of their live-space," suggested Red. The proper part, he thought – the clever caused-by-the-Power-of-the-Hand part – must be beyond the dark clump of forest and the yellow and green hill behind.

"Can you three fly as far as the shore?" Lou's dag asked anxiously, peering at them through a sail-hole.

"Of course we can," said Rampant stiffly. "But is it safe? I don't want any trouble from your kind."

"There won't be," Killdragon assured him.

The smaller boat with all the uprights in it put to sea, and soon the catamaran was deserted except for the dragons. They continued to watch through their sail-holes as the little boat went ashore and all the uprights clambered out. They kept a sharp lookout for a signal to them to fly over, but they had a long wait.

The first thing that happened was that a lot of uprights came out of the not-clever built-things and stood around in the open. Killdragon climbed onto something, and the dragons could see him waving his arms towards the wet-floater.

"At least," said Rampant, "they're actually having a heads-together."

"If *that's* what they call a heads-together, I wouldn't like to see them having a quarrel," said Perilous, because the other peepuls were now also waving their arms excitedly. Many faces kept turning towards the boat, but of course they couldn't see the dragons under the sail, which lay over them, heavy, hot and uncomfortable, and the dragons couldn't guess what was behind their faces.

At long last, Killdragon left the crowd and climbed onto a sort of path that stretched a short way out into the water, held up by bits of trees, Red reckoned. Lou's dag walked to the end of it and waved his arms in the air.

"*Now* what's he doing?" asked Rampant, straining to see through his sail-hole.

"Signalling," replied Red excitedly. "I think ... yes – he wants us to fly over!"

Red made a move to scramble out from under the sail, but his dag gave him a sharp tug with his teeth.

"Wait! How can you be sure?"

"I just am," he said.

"Well, *I* can't see them," grunted Rampant. "And those I do see, I don't trust."

Nevertheless, the dragons crawled out from under the sail and, being careful to balance the boat, stood, one full-grown on each side and Red in the middle. As soon as they appeared, the crowd of uprights on the island immediately froze.

"Now what?" Rampant muttered.

"I think they're just surprised," said Red.

"Surprised?" his mag said, shaking her head. "That's not surprise. That's terror."

But there was no way back now; there was nothing for it but to spread their wings.

This was going to be difficult, with no run and no height to jump off, but Red remembered his flying lessons and beat his wings hard enough to take him almost straight up, high enough so his tail was clear of the water.

And then he headed for the land.

He was nearly there, when he heard a cry and a loud splash from behind. He twisted his neck to look back and saw his mag floundering in the water. Her front paws were splashing, her wings uselessly beating up foam, and her head was writhing on her desperately stretching neck.

There was no doubt about it – Perilous was sinking!

CHAPTER 25

Rampant swooped down. Red turned in mid-air and raced back. They both reached Perilous at the same time. Rampant, hovering on frenziedly beating wings, dangled his tail, and Perilous, in her struggle to keep her head above water, seized it with her teeth. Red saw his dag give an agonized jerk, but he kept his wings beating, and began towing her towards the shore.

Red *had* to help!

He tried to get his head under his mag's jaw to hold her up, but as he lost height, he found he couldn't keep himself in the air. First his tail, then his back feet trailed in the water. No matter how hard he flapped them, his wings couldn't hold him up. In a flash of terror he crash-landed, back feet first, right on top of his mag.

For a moment, he felt safe with her solid back underneath him. But he knew he mustn't weigh her down – she might pull his dag's tail right off! He rolled and landed with a great splash on his side, and at once sank like a rock.

Through his terror he remembered to close his mouth and nostrils, but that was all he could do. The water bubbled in his ears, and he could see the blue-green world around him, his mag sinking beside him, his dag's tail, pulled taut, in her jaws.

Then she let it go.

They slid down the endless dark green together. Red was so frightened he couldn't feel his fear. His think-space was blank, except for one certain think: this was life-over!

Then, somehow, in all the blackness and cold, he heard Lou's words: *angels and*— What *was* it? But even that little bit helped. After the first numbness of panic, instinct made him struggle. Thrashing his front paws and kicking his back legs against the swallowing depths, Red felt himself rise and rise, until it became lighter, and fear floated away.

Then, quite suddenly, he saw his mag beside him. She too was kicking and thrashing. Both their heads broke the surface at once, and they sucked in great gulps of air. Red could feel it hit his chest-fire, and

a blast of heat filled his body with energy. He let out
a gust of steam and, with his neck at full stretch out of
the water, paddled furiously.

"Mag!" he cried. "MAG!"

"Fer-Fer…" Perilous tried to answer, but the water
in her mouth was bubbling up, making her splutter
violently.

"Don't talk, Mag! Breathe – breathe deep! We're
floating!"

Red kicked his back feet and swirled his tail as he'd
seen the sand-flappers do. He held his breath as long
as possible, then let it out quickly, and took another.
He looked ahead. The land-lump had got closer!

His mag was pressing down on the water with
her wings, which seemed to keep her afloat.

For a moment, he thought that a cloud was passing, blocking out the light-shine, but no – it was the spread of massive wings beating frantically overhead as Rampant flew over them all the way. His tail, with teeth marks visible and red-wet dripping, dangled just above them, in case they needed it.

By the time they reached shore, Red had almost stopped being afraid and had begun to enjoy whatever it was he was doing. Could this be what the sand-flappers did? Oh, but it was so exhausting!

He and his mag crawled up onto the sand, hardly noticing the crowd of uprights standing along the shore watching them in breath-stopped silence. Lou was there, and her dag, hopping about, looking as if they wanted to help the two dragons ashore but not knowing how.

Rampant curved down, his shadow falling on the uprights, making them cower. He landed heavily on the sand near by, and the peepuls scattered. He scanned the scene for a moment and spotted Perilous, still lying on her front, wet wings spread. He hurried to her.

"I'm sorry – so sorry!" she gasped. "I don't know what happened. I just couldn't stay up there…"

"It's all right, dear; it's all right now!" Rampant

kept saying, and he licked her face and patted her, and covered her tenderly with one wing.

Meanwhile, Lou was hugging Red – *really* hugging him.

"Red! I'm so glad you made it! I thought dragons couldn't swim!"

"Is *that* what I was doing?"

"Yes, and brilliantly, too. I thought you were going to drown."

"So did I," said Red, catching his breath. "But the angels saved me."

"Angels? What angels? Oh! You mean Shakespeare's!"

"Yes, those ones." Then Red added, "What *are* angels?"

"Well, they've got bodies, like me, and – and they've got wings, like you."

Red's ears pricked up. "Then … then they must be part dragon and … and part upright?"

There was a pause while Lou thought about that.

"Yes," she said at last. "That's *exactly* what angels are."

CHAPTER 26

Lou led Red to her home, leaving his mag and dag on the beach with Killdragon, surrounded by the crowd of uprights. They all wore the surprised-upright look, which didn't suggest to Red that his parents were in any danger.

It was a built-thing, but nothing like Red had expected; small, with walls and branches on top. Its mouth had straight sides – like the one in his school – which Red could hardly squeeze through. When he did, he stopped and looked round. Compared with a cave it wasn't large, but it had, through a sort of hole in the middle of the wall, a view of the beach.

He noticed there were sleeping places on tree legs with soft stuff on them and other things he'd seen in the town-place. But now he knew that uprights didn't crouch or eat off the floor, he guessed what these were for. There were many other trappings he didn't recognize or see any use for. As he pointed a few out, Lou explained.

"Those are called *pots* and *pans* – and this is a *cup*, for drinking out of." She demonstrated by lifting it to her lips, and tilting her head back.

These were made of different stuff. Causing them must have needed a lot of cleverness but the whole place seemed very flimsy compared with a cave whose solid walls always brought dragons a sense of comfort, or with his school built-thing, and those others they'd seen in the ruined town-place.

Overall Red felt quite numb with disappointment. But Lou seemed proud of it, and he soon found out why.

"My dad built this place," she explained. "He made everything: our beds, and the tables and chairs." Luckily she pointed, so Red learned the words for these things as she went along.

"*Beds ... tables ... chairs...*" he repeated. He liked *house* best.

"My mum wove all the cloth for our clothes and the bedding and curtains and everything," said Lou, continuing to point. "See this?"

"Sweater?" There was Red's very first upright word. He liked saying it.

"Yes, my mum spun the wool herself and knitted it for me. I helped her as much as I could…" Lou's voice trailed off. She fell silent, and her face changed, taking on that sad look.

"Where is your … *mum*?" Dragonsense told him this meant the same as mag.

"She died," Lou said.

"Life-over?"

"Yes."

"It wasn't—?"

"A dragon? No. It wasn't that. It was an accident."

If it had been a dragon, Red thought, she could never have forgiven them, as he could never have forgiven an upright for hurting his mag. He gave a little sigh of relief.

Lou showed him more objects with colours on them. He didn't know what these were for, but he could see that causing them must have been difficult, even for an upright.

"The clay helps – we've plenty of that. Our potters make all our dishes and things from it. As long as we've got enough trees to heat the kiln."

Red didn't bother to ask what a *kiln* was; there was already too much to take in. He looked around again, seeing it with new eyes, and suddenly it wasn't poor and sad any more, but an absolute marvel; every bit of it proved the Power of the Hand. But more than that: to have thinks before you caused things? To see them behind your eyes, plan, and then make them happen? What a wonder!

"Let me show you the garden," Lou said, leading Red outside.

Behind the house was an open space with things growing in it. Red thought, looking at the rows of different kinds of green-feed, how his dag would revel in so many different tastes. The strangest part was the flowers, which made an edge of blazing colours. That hadn't just *happened*. It had been *caused* – a pic-tur, alive and beautiful.

What was the tail-point of them, Red wondered, when you couldn't eat them? Yet this too filled him with a mixture of admiration and alarm. These uprights were not only clever, but they were also constantly puzzling. If you couldn't understand them, how could you ever reach an agreement with them?

"Those trappings – inside your *house* – did your family cause all of them?"

"Most. But not the metal things. We found those on the mainland. To make those you need tools."

"Tooooools…"

"Yes, and they're really hard to find. Even when you do find them, they're usually rusty and useless." She took a few more steps, then stopped.

"For a long time no one dared to go back in case there were dragons waiting on the cliffs. Then they began to make short trips – they had to – and found there were no dragons anywhere near the shore." Lou paused for a moment. The next part was hard to say. "Then one search party went too far in – a few miles, maybe – and…"

"What?" asked Red.

"They never came back. The story is, they ran into some dragons and—"

"We rip-burn-killed them!" Red said excitedly, but Lou's face made him realize he'd said something bad. "Sorry," he muttered.

Lou turned to him, her voice imploring. "Oh, Red! If dragons and humans could just understand each other – if they could just forgive each other; if they could see that the world could be beautiful and clean and good again. Not apart, like now, but *together*!"

"You mean griffilin!"

"What's *griffilin*?"

"It's the impossible think," he replied, and shook his head when she pressed him to say more.

The two of them stood side by side, her hand on his neck, not talking, just looking at the sweet, blazing growing things, each busy with their own thinks.

Then Lou said, "Come on, let's go back inside. I want to show you something special."

As Lou led him back inside the house, Red noticed something. He pointed at it with his tail.

"What's that?" he asked.

"That's what I was talking about – it's one of my dad's sculptures." She picked it up and showed it to him.

Red gazed at the object. He could see it was part of a tree, rough in places and smoothly shiny in others.

"Can you see what it is?" Lou asked, but Red just stood there looking at it blankly. "It's a baby!"

"*Bay-beee?*"

"Well, not a whole one, obviously. Dad says it's as if the baby's hidden – you know, in the piece of wood. He was trying to free it."

As Red had no think for what *baby* meant, let alone looked like, it was hard for him to make sense of it. But by cocking his head, first to one side and then to the other, he finally saw that some of the tree had been taken away to show part of a little animal with a big head without fur on it and a rounded belly.

"He made it when I was born," Lou said proudly. "It's me!"

"What does *born* mean?"

"Born. You know – when you first come into the world. When you arrive—"

"When you're hatched!"

"Yes, that's right."

Then it hit him. This funny little thing must be what Lou had looked like when she'd first come out of her egg! Or did uprights come out of trees?

He looked again. Yes – it could be a hatchling upright. He could make out its head, eyes closed, looking very … Red couldn't think of the right word. Something that meant so new and so soft and bare that anything could hurt it. If it were real even a mumbo could easily swallow it up in one gulp. Back in the Old Time they probably had!

Just the think of it frightened – no, revolted – him.

He tore his eyes away from the carving and looked around to distract himself. Now he noticed several other *sta-toos*. It wasn't clear what they were, but he thought he saw several different living things among them: sky-flappers, ground-runners and…

"What's *that*?"

"Not a statue."

"What, then?"

She sighed. "It's a gun."

"*Guuun…* What's it for?"

"You don't want to know."

"Yes, I do."

"Red. It's for fighting. My mum hated it, but Dad said we needed it – in case."

"In case what?"

She looked at the floor. "In case dragons ever came here. He says we have to be able to defend ourselves."

"With *that* little thing?" Red shook his head dismissively. "That's not going to help."

She looked at him. "Believe me, it could."

Down on the beach, the heads-together had begun. Perilous and Rampant were crouched on the sand; Killdragon was sitting next to them. The rest of the uprights were gathered in a half-circle opposite. If they had been able to read upright faces better, the dragons would have known their old enemies were not at all pleased to see them.

"Why did you come?" asked one, an old male. "You shouldn't have; there's nothing here for you."

"He's right," said another, a female. "You're the enemy, remember? Or have you forgotten, safe and warm and fat on our land!"

Rampant glanced at his pair, then back at the uprights. Despite wanting to open his jaws wide and consume them all in blasting gouts of flames, he remained very dragonlike: calm, decent and polite. Without saying anything, he put his snout into his pouch and drew out the precious Block of Knowledge and dropped it on the sand.

Everyone gazed in silence. There were whispers; fingers pointed.

"We've brought this Block of Knowledge to you – a very, very long way – as a signal of good thinks."

There were more agitated whispers from the uprights, then shouts.

"What's he talking about?"

"Get them off our island!"

Killdragon raised a hand for silence. After a few moments, a hush fell again.

"Listen, everyone stay calm. These dragons don't mean us any harm; they've come in peace – in *peace*." There were angry murmurs. "I made a deal with them. We need access to the mainland, and they've promised to give it to us – if we give them coal in return."

"Coal?" said the old male. "What do these blockheads want with coal?"

Suddenly a younger one stood up. "This is all nonsense! We'll give you till noon to clear off!"

This male held something in his hand. A stick of some kind? It only took Rampant a moment to recognize it: it was the same thing that one of the uprights had used to put a searing hole in him back on the mainland.

The black dragon jumped up and reared before the crowd, bellowing, "PUT THAT THING DOWN! DO IT OR I'LL STOP BEING POLITE!"

Back at Lou's house, bemused by so many new things and words, Red spotted something he recognized.

"Blocks of Knowledge!"

There, on a strip of wood resting on two big stones, were blocks – *books*. Red jumped closer to look. He lowered his snout.

"Don't touch!" Lou almost shouted.

Red gave a start. He wasn't used to that tone in her voice. She sounded like one of his teachers when someone in class said something rude.

"Can I look?"

Lou nodded nervously.

Red was surprised at the state of them. They looked

like last year's leaves off the biggest trees, somehow stuck together, with ragged, crackly-looking edges. Despite the warning, he reached out his tongue to explore them.

Lou threw herself in front of him. "I said *don't touch*!"

"Why not?"

"Because you might damage one. They're old and fragile and—" She paused and took a deep breath. "We have to be very, very careful with them. A lot of our books have fallen apart. When that happens, we have a sort of funeral for them."

"*Fyou-ner-ral?*"

"Yes, like when someone dies – life-over, you know." Red looked puzzled, so she added, "When we can't read them any more – that's the worst thing – we take them out to sea in boats and scatter the poor crumbling pages on the water."

"What for?"

"We send their stories off to places we could never reach. Then all we have left of them is what we've memorized."

"But Blocks of Knowledge have never been *alive*, so how can they reach life-over?"

Lou leaned forward, her voice trembling. "Books are the most alive things in the whole world. They can be passed down from person to person for hundreds of years. And even after they crumble away, so long as you've got them memorized, the stories can live on and on – for ever... When I have children, they'll learn them too." She reached out a finger and let it hover over one of the thicker books. "But no one can memorize all of them. It's too hard. So we copy them."

"*Copy?*"

"Yes. With pens and ink. Trouble is, in the end you run out of paper. There aren't enough trees around here."

"Has your dag used them all to make babies?"

Lou's mouth dropped open, and she made the laugh noise. As Red watched her, he wished he could join in – but laughing just wasn't a dragon thing. Instead he had a sudden flashing think: so this was why the Council had made his dag bring the Block of Knowledge. They must have known, or maybe guessed, how important books were to uprights!

Then Lou said, "Your dad's – *dag's* – book, the one he showed us, was in very good condition compared with ours."

"Con-dish-un?"

"Not ready, you know, for a funeral."

Red had to think for a moment. "Maybe because they're kept in the Special Place."

"What's that?"

"It's an old built-thing with lots of Blocks of Knowledge on wooden pieces – like you have here."

Lou's eyes widened. "A room full of books? Then – I don't believe it! – you must have a library!" Red shrugged, uncomprehending. "These books you've got, are they all like the one I saw? I mean, in such good condition?"

"I think so."

Lou gave a deep sigh. "You're *so* lucky…" She turned to him and seized one of his paws. "Red! When you get home, promise to take care of them. Every single one! Promise you'll make the other dragons understand how incredibly precious they are."

Red looked into her beseeching eyes.

"I promise," he said, even though, secretly, he felt a twinge of guilt promising anything to an upright, especially about something as important as Blocks of Knowledge. Then he added, "I wish books would talk to *me*."

"They could. I just have to teach you how to read."

He looked at her curiously. "Would you?"

"Of course. If you learn to read, books can talk to you all the time." She stopped suddenly. "I can't bear to think that dragons have all these books and can't read them. While ours are all *dying—*"

"HURRY!"

Killdragon's voice interrupted their conversation. Red could see him through the hole in the wall, charging up from the beach, his face red and shiny, and with a look on it that Red hadn't seen before – a look that alarmed him. He yelled again, waving his hands frantically.

"You have to leave – RIGHT NOW!"

CHAPTER 27

Red and Lou exchanged shocked looks. Leave? thought Red. But we've only just got here!

A moment later, Killdragon burst in, panting.

"They had a meeting – right there on the beach. They won't let you stay."

"Why not?" Red asked.

"Because you're the enemy."

Fear made the scales on Red's back stand out, and a gush of black smoke rushed from his nostrils. Lou began to cough.

"No, Dad!" she spluttered. "Make them understand they're our friends!"

"I tried. They've gone for their weapons. We must get the dragons away. Red! Go on!"

Red didn't hesitate. Something told him the parents he thought were safe were now in terrible danger. He jumped out through the mouth of Lou's home, and she and her dag hurried after him.

Red moved so fast he had to spread his wings for balance, and soon he could see his mag and dag down near the water. They were alone now, craning their necks and scouring the landscape for their son. When they saw him, they waved their tails and sent up smoke signals of relief and urgency.

"What happened, Dag?" Red exclaimed as he reached the water's edge.

"Just what I *knew* would happen. They didn't listen!"

"How are we supposed to go anywhere now?" put in Perilous. "There's no way off this stinking land-lump!"

Rampant turned furiously on Killdragon, his voice a low, menacing growl. "Your mumbo said there was coal here. That's why we came. WHERE IS IT?"

"There's no time for that now; it's almost noon! Please – you *must* go! The others will be back soon. With guns!"

"I should have listened to my dragonsense! Make a deal? With an *upright*? BAH!" The black dragon tossed his giant head this way and that, outraged.

"Rampant's right!" growled his pair. "We should never have come here to this – this faraway wretched place. How could *you* help us? You can't even help yourselves!"

Killdragon, chest heaving, took a deep breath. "There's a chance I could still change their minds," he said, glancing over his shoulder in nervous anticipation. He didn't really believe it, though. It would only be a matter of time before the other villagers arrived, with more weapons. They hadn't been at all interested in making a deal with the dragons. They just wanted them off the island. At any cost.

"Flaming uprights!" Rampant bellowed, and he reared up on his back legs, making himself so tall and terrifying that Killdragon fell over in the sand. The black dragon threw his head back and roared, "YOU WANT WAR? I'LL GIVE YOU WAR!"

He blew out a gout of flame – so hot and powerful that it exploded in a huge ball of fire.

"No, Dag!" Red cried.

"Please!" Lou begged, and burst into tears, crouching next to her dag and burying her face in his chest.

Perilous alone stayed calm. "This may be a good moment to remind you, Rampant," she said sternly, "we are *dragons*. And dragons DON'T DO WAR!"

Rampant crouched back down, snorting and

fidgeting, trying to calm his think-space enough to listen to her.

"Let's head to the top of that hill. We'll take off from there," she said.

Killdragon looked up at the sky. The sun was climbing. Soon it would be right overhead, and that would mean...

"You'd better hurry. I'll show you the quickest way."

"You still expect us to listen to *you*?" scoffed Rampant, feeling another rush of heat from his chest-fire. "Even if we manage to take off, it's much too far to fly back!" He pawed the ground, leaving deep claw marks. Killdragon stared down at them, imagining the same marks scoring the flesh on his back.

"Then we take a stand!" said Perilous. She put her head back and bellowed – as she'd hoped she'd never have to – "COME ON, UPRIGHTS! COME AND FIGHT!"

"Dad!" cried Lou. "Tell them to stop! Tell them to listen! We can't lose any more people." She turned hopefully to Red. "You said dragons don't fight!"

Red stood there, his mouth opening and closing, looking for the right words. But he couldn't find them. Then he turned to his parents.

"Mag! Dag! Lou's right, dragons DON'T fight! You've told me that all my life."

Rampant swung round to face his mumbo, eyes blazing. "That was before an upright with a terrible name persuaded us to cross the Endless Water to a flame-forsaken land-lump populated by uncivilized uprights who are RIGHT NOW preparing to end us!"

Silence.

Then, incredibly, Killdragon got to his feet and took a step towards the full-growns towering before him. Whatever fear he'd felt had been replaced by something more powerful: a genuine desire to help his ancient enemy.

"You *must* listen," he pleaded. "I know a way. If you go to the top of the hill and fly off – not the way we came, but the other direction – you'll reach land much sooner."

"Land?" Lou said, flashing her dag a puzzled look.

"There are islands – *atolls*, we call them – with no one living on them. I think you'll find coal there, too. Trust me."

There was a sound from the line of bushes and trees, some way back from the water. And suddenly—

Out they came! Uprights, holding what looked

from a distance like sticks, pointing them at the
dragons. Lou gave a cry and turned to Red.

"Don't stand there, Red! Fly! Fly! They've got guns!"

Lou was frantic. She tried to push the dragons – first
Red, then the other two – towards the big hill. She
couldn't budge Perilous or Rampant, of course, but
Red she could move a little.

"Quick, get away!" she cried.

Rampant looked at the hill and then back at the
approaching uprights, then at Killdragon.

"Tell me more about these *aaa-tols*," he said.

"You have to think of them like – like stepping
stones. You fly to the first and rest. Then you fly to
the second and do the same, and so on and so on until
you reach the mainland."

"But…" Red looked out at the Endless Water, past
the wet-floater to the horizon. "The mainland's that
way, where we came from."

"There's more than one mainland!" shouted
Killdragon. "For all our sakes, leave now! Go!" He
took a step towards Rampant. "If you don't, they'll
kill you all."

Suddenly they heard a number of loud bangs, followed by sounds like furry-buzzers.

"Go!" Lou urged. "Before it's too late!"

There was no time for a heads-together; so, faced with guns and that many angry uprights, Rampant made his decision.

"DRAGONS – JUMP FOR YOUR LIVES!"

Rampant started up the hill, his pair at his side, Red close behind. There was no time to say goodbye to the little upright.

It was hard to jump uphill, very hard, and Red didn't dare to stop to try to take off. His mag and dag were having trouble too, especially Rampant.

"We're not ... jumping ... fast enough!" he gasped.

BANG! BANG! BANG!

More shots rang out, missing them but driving them on. Red could hear angry shouts behind them, and he could feel the vibrations of pursuing feet. Getting closer.

He glanced back just long enough to take in the faces of their pursuers: female and male uprights, pointing their sticks and urging one another forward.

With every breath he took, Red could feel his firebox getting hotter.

Suddenly, among all the other yelling voices, came Lou's. She was right behind him.

"GO ON, RED, GO ON!"

Red knew his mag and dag couldn't jump fast enough to reach the top of the hill before the angry peepuls caught up – or their furry-buzzers, which moved much faster than they did. He had to do something to hold off the pursuit somehow.

Suddenly it was as if his think-space emptied of fear and filled up with something else. There were words for it that he'd never been allowed to use. He put back his head, opened his throat and—

ROOOOAAAAAARRR!

After the roar, there was a sudden rush – and a flame streamed out. He felt it shoot across his tongue and fizz between his teeth. It shocked and thrilled him at the same time. He'd only ever breathed one little flame before, and never like this. But now, threatened, and his mag and dag's last hope, he found that he could.

He turned back to face the angry crowd.

Flames flowed freely now, blasting from his jaws

down the hill, stopping his pursuers in their tracks. Several, feeling the searing heat, dropped their weapons and put their hands up to shield their faces.

"STAY BACK!" Red roared. "STAY BACK OR I'LL RIP-BURN-KILL YOU!"

His voice too had changed. It was no longer a mumbo's. Too deep, too furious. His think-space emptied of every decent think, leaving only one terribly indecent one – the one his granddag had told him about.

VIOLENCE.

He didn't know that behind him, higher up the hill, Rampant and Perilous had turned and were gazing

down at their mumbo, jaw-smacked. While he stood there, wreathing his neck and feeling his eyes growing hot, he saw Killdragon, with Lou beside him, running straight at the crowd, waving them away and yelling.

"Stop! Let them go! It isn't noon yet – it still isn't noon!"

The crowd stopped. It was a moment when anything might happen.

And then something did. The last thing Red would ever have expected. A great winged shadow spread itself over the scene. It grew bigger and blacker. Before Red's next breath, Lou, who'd been at her dag's side …

… was gone!

Red twisted his neck, staring upward. His dag had taken off from higher up, swooped down, and snatched Lou in his jaws. And now Rampant was carrying her – helpless, kicking and screaming – back up the hill to the very top and over and beyond and out of sight.

The little dragon, shocked almost beyond movement, somehow found the strength to beat his wings and rise. As he did, he heard more gun-noises followed by the buzzing sound and then something hot tore through his wing. At the same time, he saw his mag jump along the crest of the hill and launch herself off. As Red felt the wind passing through the burning hole in his wing, costing him some height, he glanced back down the hill.

Below was Killdragon, standing in front of the crowd, gazing up at Rampant. He put both front legs to the sides of his head and let out an agonized howl.

"NOOOO! NOT MY GIRL! BRING HER BACK. BRING HER *BACK*!"

CHAPTER 28

Red flew away across the Endless Water, leaving the uprights shouting and firing their weapons behind. It wasn't long before he'd caught up with his dag and could see Lou dangling from his huge jaws. She wasn't struggling and screaming any more. She just hung, her arms and legs swaying limply. He couldn't tell if she was alive or – what was her word? – *dead*.

He flew closer.

He could see better now. If his dag bit down on Lou's body, he'd cut her in half. But those powerful jaws could be perfectly controlled. Red knew this because his dag had often picked him up as a hatchling. Then his teeth hadn't left so much as a scratch on his skin – his thick *dragon* skin. But what of Lou's, so thin and scaleless? How could those teeth not pierce *her*? Looking past the wide flapping wings that kept blocking his view, Red could see no red-wet.

Oh, Dag, he thought. Be careful with her!

The hole in his wing still hurt, the edges blown hot by the wind. Red's think-space hurt too, but not for himself. It was for Lou's dag, and how he must feel. It was like having a black pain-filled hole – *deep inside*. And that one, to his surprise, hurt even more.

He focused his thinks on flying his best and his furthest.

For many warms and colds, dragons had been able to fly far. They flew all over the world. But as they slowly settled, their natural curiosity faded too. For generations, safe in their live-places, they convinced themselves they had everything they needed. Until the coal threatened to run out. But, just as uprights can do desperate deeds of strength when they must, so too can dragons.

Rampant and his family were proof of this.

With the sea stretching endlessly beneath them, they flew as they'd never known they could fly. Lou's body, though not heavy, made Rampant's trial far greater. Several times he nearly dropped her – not because he had to but because of a gnawing feeling in his think-space that she didn't deserve to be carried. He suspected she'd lied – or her shell-cracker of a dag. He'd grabbed her on an impulse, propelled by a flash of anger, pure and simple, against Killdragon. *Killdragon* – what a name! But as he flew, on the verge of dropping her, one think stopped him: she might be useful.

They flew until light-shine started to fade without any sign of land. Not a solitary dot against the endless blue. Their wings were aching; their bodies seemed to be getting heavier and heavier, pulling them towards the sea. They all shared the same fearful think: when the light-shine goes down and stops warming us, we'll lose the strength to stay flying. Then we'll fall – down, down, down – into the Endless Water. Even if we managed to stay afloat for a little while, it would soon be life-over!

They flew lower and lower until Rampant's tail and Lou's feet were trailing in the waves. Perilous was almost at her last gasp. Then Red, who was flying above them now, suddenly let out a cry.

"Dag! Mag! Look! There's something ahead!"

With super-dragon effort, his dag pumped his wings and rose a little. Perilous stretched her exhausted neck. As they did, they saw what Red had seen.

Something in the water big enough for them to land on.

A tiny land-lump!

The sight was enough to summon a final effort from all of them. In another few moments of desperate, laboured wing strokes, their feet touched down on something solid. The relief!

But it wasn't a land-lump. It sloped away on either side from a central ridge, and it moved uneasily with the motion of the sea. Once they'd carefully made a balanced landing, however, it was wide enough for them to spread themselves across the ridge for the most desperately needed rest of their lives.

They lay there, exhausted.

Lou lay there too, spat out of jaws that could no longer hold her. Red, opening his eyes with great difficulty, saw her sprawled a little way from him, quite still. He looked anxiously but could see no tooth-holes on her body. He crawled closer, then touched her with his tongue. She stirred, blinked, and managed a tired smile.

"Red..." she whispered.

"We did it," he whispered back, and spread a wing over her to keep her warm.

Dark came. The two exhausted full-growns
slept without dreams, but Lou dreamed, and, most
unusually for dragons, so did Red.

Lou dreamed she was on the mainland, in the
world of dragons. She was holding her favourite book,
The Complete Works of Shakespeare, to her chest.
Everything around her was huge, even the trees and
flowers and birds; she was frightened, and kept calling
for her dad. He didn't come, and she felt desolate and
abandoned.

In her head was this phrase: *Farewell! God knows
when we shall meet again.* She'd learned Juliet's whole

speech without wondering who God was. Now she wondered. Suddenly Red was beside her, gently puffing white smoke in her ear, and telling her not be scared. But she *was* scared. Things kept getting bigger and bigger until only she and Red were small and alone together in a looming world of giants.

Perhaps because of the sound of the sea in his sensitive ears, Red's dream was different. In it, he and Lou were swimming underwater. But it wasn't a roaring, dark, drowning place like before; it was a wonderful, bright, quiet world, a bit like her garden. There were forests of shimmering plants and many beautiful sea creatures who didn't mind them being in their silent, radiant home. All the fearful, confusing things had been left behind. In a world like this, he and Lou could be friends without it mattering that their kinds were enemies.

Meanwhile, in the *real* world, the dark sea rocked them on their strange moving *something*. None of them knew it was carrying them nearer and nearer to a land mysterious to them all. A place where anything might happen.

CHAPTER 29

Red was first to wake. As his eyes blinked against the sharp rays of morning light, he could see something looming on the edge of the sea. Black at first. But then his vision adjusted. He rose onto his haunches and gazed. And now he could see what it was.

Land!

Excitedly he jumped about, waking the others. He wanted to tell his dag, to celebrate – but something stopped him. Now that he was no longer worried about Lou, his think-space filled with angry thinks about his dag, and the terrible thing he'd done.

His mag was angry too, but she knew she had to take charge. She turned her back on her pair and clacked her wings towards him to show her displeasure. Rampant huffed dismissively.

"Now then, young ones," Perilous said briskly. "We've got to get off this land-lump."

"It isn't a land-lump," said Lou, stretching and yawning. "It's an upside-down ship."

There was an awkward silence while the three dragons looked around them. By light, they could see she was right.

"What's *up-si-dow*?" asked Red, ever curious.

"Like this." Lou showed them by turning her hand the other way up.

"How did that happen?" asked Perilous.

Lou shrugged. "Don't know. Maybe it ran into a storm and capsized."

Red didn't know that word, and he didn't like the sound of it.

"It's much bigger than the big wet-floater," observed Perilous. "Even with the Power of the Hand, how could anyone cause something so big?"

"By using *many* hands," said Lou. "By working together, and probably with the help of machines."

"What are *ma-sheeens*?" asked Red.

"They're things; things that do what hands do – but faster. They're a lot stronger, too."

"Stronger than a *dragon*?" Red asked.

"Some of them."

The dragons exchanged doubtful looks.

Then Perilous shook herself. "Whoever or *whatever* caused it, we're lucky we found it. But right now, we have to reach land and find food and a liveplace."

"I'm not going anywhere till Dag explains," said Red firmly.

Rampant, perched silently on the ridge, stood up and half spread his wings. He looked huge and black and fierce. The sight of him made Lou shrink behind Red. But the full-grown's anger was not directed at her. It was directed at his son.

"How DARE you talk to me like that! I'm your dag, and DON'T YOU FORGET IT!"

Red was rattled but he stood his ground. "I want to know why you took Lou."

"Yes, Rampant," Mag broke in. "That wasn't decent and it certainly wasn't sensible."

There was a pause.

"Why? *Why?*" Rampant growled. "Because that little shell-cracker's dag LIED TO US!" He turned to Lou. "And you KNEW it!"

Red looked away, shocked. Shell-cracker? That was beyond rude! It meant a mumbo who comes out of its egg too early. A deeply shameful thing.

"He knew there were no *aaa-tols*." Despite himself, Rampant was learning upright words too. "He tricked us – first into coming back with him, and again by sending us out here to nothing! He doesn't care if we drown. So I took her—"

"Hostage!" Lou shouted. A sudden surge of defiance made her emerge from behind Red. "My dad was trying to keep you from being killed. He just wanted to help!"

There was a tense pause.

Rampant's belly heaved up and down, as if his chest-fire was expanding inside him. As if he might just throw his head back, like before, and send out a scorching flame at Lou—

"Look! Look! I think there's an atoll!" shouted Red. They all looked.

"That's not an atoll," Lou said. "That's the mainland."

From the upside-down ship the shore seemed close. But getting there proved harder than any of them expected. Though Rampant had so far protected Lou from his teeth by some clever use of his long tongue, she refused to be carried in his jaws again.

Relieved of the burden, Rampant flew to shore without difficulty, followed closely by Perilous. They both assumed that their son would follow. After all, weren't uprights perfectly good swimmers? It wasn't until they'd landed on the beach that they realized Red and Lou weren't coming. They blew agitated smoke signals towards him, but Red stayed where he was.

"Why doesn't he come?" Rampant growled.

"Because he's a dragon – he won't leave her."

"He's just like his granddag," Rampant muttered. "A born rebel." Despite himself, he silently admired him for it. They stared out at the not-atoll and hoped their mumbo had a plan.

When Red suggested he carry her to shore, Lou dismissed the idea.

"No need," she replied. "It's not far; I can swim."

Red glanced over at the water which seemed to stretch some distance before the break-water.

"Are you sure?"

"If there's one good thing about living on an island, it's that you learn to swim before you can walk. I'll be fine, especially if you fly over me and leave your tail dangling – just in case."

Red helped her down the slippery side of the boat into the sea. She slid so fast that she lost control and fell into the deep water, vanishing from sight. But before he could blow a puff of panic-smoke, he saw bubbles rising, and her head popped out.

"I'm all right!" she shouted, and began swimming strongly for shore.

Red, hovering above her, watched, fascinated, how she moved her legs, scooping and kicking. It surprised him that, instead of swimming under the water like a sand-flapper, she kept her head high and sucked in air, as he'd had to do. While he was watching, and thinking that his parents would probably rip-burn-kill him for ignoring their signals, he noticed something.

A dark shape in the water.

It was circling Lou, and getting closer. What was it? A sand-flapper, probably curious about her, Red thought.

"Look!" he shouted gleefully. "You've got a swim-friend!"

Lou's head snapped round to where Red's tail was pointing. At that moment, the swell lifted her, and she saw what every islander feared …

… a black fin cutting through the water straight towards her!

"*Sh-sh-shaaark!*" She tried to scream the word, but it got strangled in her throat.

"What did you say?" Red called down curiously.

But when he saw her suddenly stop swimming and start splashing the water with her hands, dragonsense took over. After a last frantic glance at him, Lou sucked in air and dived straight down to escape. He saw the *sh-sh-shaaark* go under after her, with a flick of its powerful tail. The creature's life-over-bringing jaws were almost at Lou's body when, at the last moment—

Red seized its tail in his own jaws, driving his teeth through its rough flesh. Its whole body was jerked backwards and hoisted out of the sea. It thrashed and snapped wildly, shaking its head, but before it could bite him it was flung violently against the side of the boat, where it fell limply back into the water, floated perfectly still for a moment, then, with a final twitch of its tail, slipped beneath the surface.

Lou, her lungs bursting, her heart threatening to burst too, shot to the surface. The first thing she saw was Red's tail, dangling just in front of her.

"Grab it!" Red shouted. "I'll pull you to shore!"

It was still quite a long way, but by Lou kicking as hard as she could, and with Red towing, they made it from the deep water, through the breakers and, with the last of their strength, dragged themselves onto the shore. Red, lying on his belly in the sand – with Lou, exhausted and gasping next to him – closed his eyes.

When he opened them again, he saw something much scarier than any shark.

"What did you think you were doing out there?" said his dag sternly.

"I – I was ending something. A giant sand-flapper that wanted to eat Lou…"

"Yes, I saw." Rampant took a step closer. "Well ended, son."

Red didn't say anything; he was too surprised. Was his dag praising him for disobeying his signals?

"Come on, killer. Get up here and give your old dag a hug!" When Red still didn't react, Rampant curled his tail around his son and pulled him to his haunches. Then he threw a wing around him and drew him in for a hug. "I'm proud of you, son!"

"I thought you were going to scorch my tail-end," murmured Red.

"I would have too, if your mag hadn't talked some dragonsense into me."

Perilous stepped forward then and nuzzled her mumbo. "I told him if anyone's going to do any tail-end scorching around here, it'll be me," she said.

Lou watched the three dragons. Despite the terror of being taken hostage and dangling from giant jaws for miles over the sea, spending a night on a capsized boat and almost being torn apart by a shark, she couldn't help noticing that her kind's sworn enemy seemed … well, amazingly, far gentler and more loving than she could have thought possible.

She watched, and wondered whether all the stories she'd heard about dragons were true. And for the very first time in her life, she doubted it.

BLOCK VIII
THE
SKYSCRAPER
PEOPLE

CHAPTER 30

Once Red and Lou had rested a bit, Lou suggested they look around for any signs of life.

"There's no trappings here, thank Flame. I've looked," Rampant told them. "Anyway, let's not forget what we're here for – coal."

There might not have been trappings, but there were trees and lots of other growing things, and some fruit that they all ate ravenously – except Perilous, who thought they were tongue-curling.

"After all I've been through," she muttered, "I need meat." And off she flew to find some.

She wasn't gone for long. She returned empty-jawed and agitated.

"Well? Did you find anything?" her pair asked.

"You're not going to like this, Rampant," she said. "I found caves – plenty of them – but I also saw" – she gave her head a shake – "built-things."

"WHAT!" Rampant reeled. Hastily he cleared his throat and tried to sound calm and in control. "Uprights may have lived here in the Old Time."

"Yes," she replied. "But these built-things were different. For a start, they're tall. One was so tall it looked like it touched the sky! You could see it from here if the trees weren't in the way."

This brought Lou to her feet. "Did you say *touching the sky*?" Perilous nodded. "Then I think I know what they are. I've seen pictures."

"What are they?" asked Red.

"They're skyscrapers."

"Sky *what*?"

"Scrapers."

The three dragons stared at her blankly. She explained.

"Long ago, when there were a lot more people and not enough space for everyone to live on the ground, they built upward – tall, tall buildings that they called skyscrapers."

"Clever..." whispered Red.

"I want to see them," said Lou firmly.

"There might still be uprights living in them – we mustn't go anywhere near them," warned Perilous.

Rampant turned and looked at her. "You've

forgotten our mission. It's to find coal and get it home.
For that we have to find uprights."

"But, Rampant, after everything they've tried to do
to us? You want to risk it?"

"D'you want to become undragoned? Because that's
what's waiting for us if we don't find coal."

There was a heavy pause.

"All right," his pair finally said. "But if we're going
to meet uprights, there might be fighting. And I'm not
doing any of that unless I've got food in my belly."

"Thank Flame!" shouted Red, jumping up and
down excitedly. "I'm at life-over from hunger!"

The dragons soon found animal tracks leading off into
the trees and scrub. They couldn't tell exactly what
had left them, but by the size and scent they knew it
was worth hunting. Under Perilous's direction, they
set off in pursuit, all of them, with Lou on Red's back,
using their sensitive dragon nostrils to follow the trail.
There was an excitement in them now, swelling like
the sounds of wildlife around them.

With every pounding step, Rampant felt his hunting
instinct returning. His mouth watered and his chest-

fire heated up, as if preparing itself to cook the meat he'd sworn he'd never eat. Hanging branches and thick brush made progress slow at times, but the full-growns swatted them away with their snouts and forepaws.

It wasn't long before they reached a clearing; and there Lou got the full-growns to dig a *pit*, as she called it, across one of the tracks. Afterwards the dragons watched, fascinated, as she broke off twigs and laid them across the hole, then put leaves on top to hide it.

"Now what?" Rampant asked wearily.

"We wait," said Lou.

The dragons and Lou waited. Then waited some more... They began to think that if they didn't eat soon, they'd reach life-over before dark. Eventually both Rampant and Perilous had to close their nostrils to shut out Lou's deliciously meaty scent which threatened to arouse their appetites and override their decency. While they lay in wait, Red turned to Lou. "Could you tell us a story?" he asked.

"Shh!" she hissed. "You'll scare the game!"

Rampant looked at her. "Is that what you call this? A GAME!" he roared.

There was a sudden wild chattering and shaking of branches above them.

"No, not *that* kind of game. I meant the animal we're trying to trap."

"No chance of that now," Red said, flashing his dag an accusing look.

"Upright words – always more upright words," muttered Rampant. "I don't understand any of them!"

"If you listened a little more and roared a little less, perhaps you would," whispered Perilous.

There was a moment of silence, enough for the din above them to calm.

Then Red said, "Maybe we should move somewhere else – where the *game* won't hear us."

So they did, Rampant huffing grumpily. But it was quite astonishing how quickly Lou took their think-spaces away from their hunger by telling them a story.

"Once upon an Old Time," she began in a hushed voice, "there was a prince called Hamlet—"

"Wait!" said Red. "What's a *prin-sss*?"

Rampant groaned. "Here we go again – more upright words."

"A prince," Lou explained, "is a very important person. Anyway, this one found out that his uncle had killed his dad by pouring poison into his ear—"

"What's *poy-zone*?"

"You know – bad stuff."

"Why? Was there a war?" asked Red.

"No…"

"You mean," said Rampant, "that an upright ended another upright – and not even in a war?"

Lou shrugged.

"What did *Ham-let* do?" asked Red. "Take it to the Council?"

"I don't think there was a council. He just, well, talked to himself a lot."

"To *himself*?" said Perilous. "Why would anyone talk to themselves?"

"Shh! Let her tell!" hissed Red.

Lou continued. "So Hamlet said, *To be, or not to be; that is the question—*"

"The question? What question?" asked Red.

Lou sighed. This was turning out to be a lot more difficult than she'd expected.

"The question – if I remember rightly – was whether he should kill his uncle or kill himself."

"How can you kill *yourself*?"

"Uprights are capable of anything," muttered

Rampant, shaking his head. "When they're not killing everything else, they're killing *themselves*!"

"Maybe uprights were like Ham-let's uncle," Red said suddenly, "pouring bad stuff into the ear of the world … and ending it."

Lou turned to him, amazed. "Red! How d'you come up with this stuff? You're so clever."

All the dragons stared at her. An *upright* praising a *dragon* – and a half-grown at that! Not for strength, not for decency. But for *cleverness*!

Just then they heard sounds – coming from the pit.

"We've caught something!" cried Red, and they all scrambled to find out what.

A fur-hopper – *rabbit*, as Lou called it – was crouched in the bottom of the hole, trembling and peering up at them.

"It worked – it really worked!" marvelled Red. He turned to Lou. "*You're* the clever one! *You* are!"

In a flash, Rampant tried to grab the fragile little creature in his jaws, but Lou's piercing voice stopped him.

"No! Don't hurt it!"

The black dragon looked at her. "*Hurt* it?" he said, baffled. "I won't hurt it. It won't feel a thing!"

But before he could do anything, Lou threw herself on the ground, reached down and picked the rabbit up by the ears. It tried to kick her, but she held it firmly, and stroked it calmingly.

"What are you doing?" asked Perilous, peering down. "You caught it and now you don't want to eat it?"

"It's just ... I've never killed anything," Lou mumbled into its soft fur. "That was always my dad's job."

"And now it's mine," said Rampant, lowering his mouth towards the creature struggling in her arms. Lou shielded the rabbit and put one hand on the dragon's huge snout.

"Please – don't hurt it!"

"OUTRAGEOUS!" Rampant growled. Suddenly he was struggling to control the hotness behind his eyes again. "Uprights," he said furiously, "especially puny little mumbos, do not come between a dragon and his prey – if they know what's good for them!"

He made another lunge for the rabbit. This time Lou swatted him on the nose. He hardly felt it, of course, but the shock made him jerk his head back and roar, just as he'd done on the beach when the uprights had attacked him. It sounded like thunder.

"HOW DAAAAARE YOU!"

This time it really looked as if he might do the unthinkable – exactly what his name suggested – and bite her head clean off.

"NO, DAG!" shouted Red. Just in time, he jumped between his dag and Lou.

Then Perilous spoke, her words loud and stern. "Rampant! You stop this nonsense at once! She's just a little thing."

"She hit me."

"Serves you right for scaring her like that!"

"She started it!"

"Will you stop being such a big whiny mumbo!" said Perilous, and she turned to Lou. "Ignore him; he's just hangry."

"Wh-what's *h-hangry*?" stammered Lou, still stroking the rabbit with trembling fingers.

"It means angry from being hungry. *There's* a good dragon word. Anyway, one little fur-hopper can't feed us all. We're going to need a bigger pit."

Lou scrambled up, shooing the terrified rabbit away. Rampant watched hungrily as it scampered off through the brush.

Meanwhile, Perilous was watching the little upright. The full-grown felt something inside, and it had nothing to do with her firebox or her empty belly. Before she knew what she was doing, she found that her wing had moved – by itself – to enfold Lou for a moment.

Suddenly the green dragon knew she'd never seen anything so sweet or so very brave as this upstart upright holding a mouthful of food – and releasing it!

Next came the most extraordinary think: was it possible that uprights, the most selfish and brutal creatures in all the world, could sometimes be unselfish and kind?

~ාංⒺ~

They switched plans from digging a bigger pit, and the group pushed on through the brush, swatting away hanging leaves and branches until they reached a clearing big enough for them to attempt a running take-off.

This time Perilous offered to carry Lou. The problem was that the full-grown's back-fins were stiff and wouldn't lie flat, so she had to carry the little upright in her forepaws. Perilous was strong, and Lou wasn't very heavy; still, they all hoped the flight wouldn't last long. As soon as they rose above the trees, the skyscrapers Perilous had described began to appear.

They landed about halfway towards the built-things, and the dragons managed without too much difficulty to catch a large animal – a kind they'd never seen before. This one didn't seem to draw the same sympathy from Lou, and when Perilous pounced on it and caused life-over in a flash of claws and teeth, the little upright just turned her head away. Later, when she was offered raw flesh, Lou refused.

"I don't eat meat like that," she said, shuddering.

"Like what?" asked Red. "It's delicious."

"We cook our food before we eat it."

The dragons looked at each other, and Rampant gave one of his usual dismissive huffs. "Uprights…" he mumbled.

The first thing Lou did was collect wood. She gathered it into a pile and then asked Red politely to light it for her with one of his flames. He obliged and the dry tinder was soon ablaze.

What she did next reminded the dragons, jarringly, of the statue of Saint George. She took her meat and stuck it on the end of a stick!

By now, dark smoke was drifting from their nostrils, but Lou didn't notice. She thrust the meat into the flames and turned it slowly until it browned. She offered a piece to Red. He glanced at his parents. His mag hesitated, then gave a little nod of assent, so he nibbled a piece before taking a bigger bite. He chewed for a moment, then looked at Lou.

"This is the tastiest thing I've ever eaten!"

"Nonsense!" scoffed Rampant.

Perilous needed no urging. Lou handed her a piece of the browned meat, and after nibbling it carefully, and then munching it, she gave her opinion.

"Cooking is an excellent think."

"Uprights don't have any excellent thinks," Rampant grunted, between more mouthfuls of raw flesh. "They should leave those to dragons."

When they'd had their fill, Perilous made her pair and son eat the blackened bits of bone and firewood. They had hardly any coal remaining. Red shared his last tiny pieces with his mag and dag, which left his pouch empty.

"If we don't find more soon," Rampant said, "you know what'll happen."

"What?" Lou asked.

There was a deathly silence.

Then Red said in a tiny voice, "It would be terrible."

"You mean – life-over?"

"Worse," grunted Rampant. "We'd be *undragoned*."

"Is being undragoned worse than dying?" asked Lou.

"It's something uprights wouldn't know about," growled Rampant. "I've got a word for you: shame. We know it doesn't mean much to *you*, but for us dragons, shame is the worst thing possible."

Lou and Red stared at each other for a moment.

Then Perilous said, "We can always eat burned bone-ends and wood," and she nuzzled her son.

"Bone-ends and wood?" said Rampant. "Those just keep the out-fires going. You can only breathe in-fires from coal."

There was more silence. Sitting there, having been accused of not knowing things when she had every right to feel angry, caused the rain to appear in Lou's eyes again. Red noticed at once.

"What's wrong?" he asked. "Are you cave-sick?"

"If you mean am I missing home, then yes, of course I am. My dad must be going crazy. He'll think I'm dead by now!" Her gaze flew to Rampant. She

opened her mouth as if to say something further, then closed it again, and hid her face in her hands.

It was hard for Red, too. After all, it was his dag's fault that she was here. And yet, despite how much it hurt inside to think of what Lou was feeling, he was glad she was there. He was glad to have a friend in this faraway place. Not to be alone with his darker thinks. As he reached out a paw to comfort her, she lifted her head and gazed at him.

"Red…"

"What?"

"You've got *your* sad face now. A sad dragon face."

"But that's—"

"IMPOSSIBLE!" Rampant boomed, spitting out pieces of flesh. "A dragon's face – as you call it – doesn't change. How can it? When we show our feelings, we show them in smoke."

"Then how did I know?" said Lou quietly.

Before anyone could answer, Rampant, now restless, wiped his snout on the long grass and stood in his commanding position. "LESS TALKING, MORE FLYING!" he roared.

When they finally found some level ground from which they could take off again, they saw they'd come a long way. The skyscrapers – their tops, at least – loomed over the trees. The tallest had a roof that came to a high point, which reminded Lou of something – some picture she'd seen of an Old Time town. She couldn't think which.

As they flew closer, Lou, dangling from Perilous's paws, saw that most, but not all, of the buildings were half collapsed or fallen completely, no more than giant piles of rubble. She stared down at them, and her mind began to race. Once these had been magnificent thriving places, filled with people, with life – she'd seen them in books. But that was long before the Dragon Wars.

They flew on, her imagination filling with dreadful sounds: cries and screams, the deafening roars of marauding dragons swooping and grabbing fleeing people in their jaws. Images of death and fire and destruction. She shut her eyes against them, feeling the wind pressing against her face, and tried to forget she was at the mercy of the very creatures who'd once laid waste to humankind.

She focused her mind on warm feelings, on her

friend Red. Wait – her *friend*? She opened her eyes briefly and looked down again and… No! How could he be that? He was the enemy – the *enemy*!

And yet … perhaps not. These weren't like the dumb, unthinking fire-breathing monsters she'd learned about. They were different. They were civilized. They were decent.

Yes, yes. They'd come a long way – such a very, very long way…

She wondered if her own kind had come as far.

CHAPTER 31

Eventually, the dragons and Lou landed in a big open space just outside the skyscraper town-place. The first thing the dragons did was to stretch their necks and sniff.

"There are dragons here," said Perilous. "I can smell them. But there's something else…"

"What is it?" hissed Rampant.

And suddenly, as if in answer, they appeared: uprights! Coming from the direction of the built-things and across the open space; a crowd of them, shouting and waving guns, and other weapons, just as Lou's peepuls had. The dragon family, shocked roarless, backed away, hissing furiously and blowing black smoke.

Lou watched the crowd thoughtfully, seemingly unafraid. Then, unlike the dragons, she moved forward to meet them. As the group drew closer, Lou greeted them, waving her hands, and smiling. And then she was face to face with one of them – the leader, maybe? From where he was standing, Red couldn't tell.

The dragons watched from a distance, eyes strained, ears pricked.

"What're they saying?" whispered Perilous.

"Can't hear; they're too far away," replied Rampant.

Red, whose burning curiosity made it impossible for him to stand still for long, moved to follow Lou. His mag tried to grab him but missed.

"No! Ferocity!"

He was off, jumping through the brush, and soon he was standing next to her. The uprights seemed agitated by his presence.

He stretched his neck to whisper into Lou's ear. "What did they say?"

"I didn't understand all of it. They're speaking with a different accent."

"What's *ack-zent*?"

"It means the same language but a different way of speaking it."

She turned from the skyscraper peepuls and led Red a little distance away. The uprights chattered and pointed, mostly at Red.

She whispered, "I asked them if there were dragons here."

"And? What did they say?"

"They said there are."

"Dag was right."

Suddenly one of the uprights – a female – crept forward, past the others. Before Red could react, she was reaching out and patting him and doing the happy-face. Red wanted to jerk his head away, but she moved her hand, as if signalling him to come closer. There were excited murmurs from the other uprights. A hush fell.

Red could feel something causing him to obey – it must be the dreaded Power of the Hand, he thought. He lowered his head. Next thing he knew, the upright was wiggling her fingers behind his ear. She began to laugh – he'd seen Lou do it enough times to know what that sounded like. Then slowly she began to say words – words he recognized – like the ones Lou had said the first time she met him on the beach.

"When th' Red Red Dragon comes out o' the sky—"

"Hey!" Lou cried. "You know the song! Our Red Dragon song!" And she joined in. *"I know that I will learn how to fly…"*

Dead silence. Then a cry went up – voices in their

277

strange *accent*. "Th' Red Dragon's come. He's come!"

After that, the uprights surged around Red, chattering and jostling one another to get closer. He tried to back away, but it was no use – they were everywhere, patting and stroking him. From where his parents were standing, there could be only one explanation: their son was under attack! They gave a joint roar and came charging across the open space.

Lou felt small and helpless, overwhelmed by the crowd all shouting and singing and trying to touch Red, knowing that any moment his furious parents would be upon them.

Suddenly, with a rattle of his scales, Red shook off the many hands, spread his wings, and did the best straight-up take-off he'd ever done – rising above the crowd, the rapid beating of his wings blowing air in their faces, making them close their eyes and turn their heads away.

Rampant and Perilous halted mid-charge and gazed up at their son. As he drew away, the uprights were no longer singing or smiling but pointing up at him.

The man Lou had spoken to shouted, "'Tis flyin', look – flyin'!"

"Of course he's flying," Lou replied. "He's a dragon!"

The man's eyes widened. He stared at her, then back up at Red, hovering above them. He turned to his fellow uprights. "It cannae be th' real Red Dragon – 'tis a trick! Run for yer lives!"

The uprights erupted, uttering more words. What *were* they saying? Lou couldn't be sure, but it seemed as if they were arguing, their voices fierce, afraid and unbelieving. Now the crowd was breaking up, streaming back towards the skyscrapers.

Suddenly an old woman grabbed the one who seemed to be in charge.

"Monolo! C'mon! Quick!" she cried, waving her free arm towards Red, dragging the leader after the others.

Lou looked around. She saw Rampant and Perilous close behind her. They too were staring up at Red, who was now some distance away, hovering skilfully over a wall of trees.

"Listen!" panted Lou. "I think these people are friendly. I don't think they want to hurt any of you."

"Didn't look that way from where I was crouching," growled Rampant.

"I think they just wanted to welcome your son."

"*Welcome* him?" said Perilous. "Why would they welcome a dragon?"

Lou shook her head. "I don't know – something to do with the song, maybe? The one we all know, about the Red Dragon."

"What's a *song*?" grunted Rampant impatiently. "And what's it got to do with our son?"

"Yes," said Perilous. "And if they're so interested, why are they all running away?"

"Because," replied Rampant, drawing his massive body to full height, "they know what's flaming well good for them!"

~✦~

Rampant watched the uprights running for their lives, hiding in the rubble or in holes in the crumbled skyscrapers on the edge of the town-place, until everyone had disappeared.

"Cowards!" he muttered, but his attention quickly returned to Red. "Did you see his lift-off?" he said to his pair. "What a flyer!" And he puffed out his dappled chest proudly.

High above them, Red was feeling quite proud of himself, too. He was scanning the view when a gust of wind brought a scent to his nostrils.

Dragons!

So close to uprights? *Couldn't* be.

A few more flaps of his wings carried him over the belt of trees and then he saw them: black, green, brown, a great gathering. His heart lifted. Odd as it was to see them here, they were his kind and he hadn't seen any others for so long. Then he noticed something strange. The dragons below were surrounded by what appeared to be high walls made of stone. He flew lower and hovered above them. Yes.

There was no doubt about it. They were shut in and crowded together in a way that dragons – the ones *he* knew – couldn't be, not by choice, at least. Red stared. And his lifted heart began to sink.

If they couldn't jump the walls or knock them down, why didn't they just fly away?

One caught sight of him. It peered and stretched its neck, as if in disbelief. Then it signalled with its tail. Others began to look up and do the same. Soon they were all signalling – but the way they signalled was smoke-stopping: by curving their tails to point at their chests. A back-think came to Red, of when his teacher had warned his class of the worst – the very worst – signal any dragon could ever make.

"Undragons..." Red whispered, unbelieving.

He didn't signal back. The think didn't occur to him. He just flapped his wings as fast as he could and hurried back to his parents and Lou. He landed quietly beside them.

"Red!" cried Lou. "You're back!"

He didn't answer her, just jumped right past to his parents. But he couldn't think what to say. How do you tell your mag and dag the worst thing possible? He had to try.

"Dag, Mag, I went exploring – and I found something."

"What?"

"Dragons."

Rampant caused a puff of dark smoke. "They must smell we're here. Why haven't they come to meet us?" Red didn't answer. "Take me to them, son."

Rampant made a move to leave, but Red stopped him.

"Wait, Dag. There's something else – something I need to tell you about them."

"What is it?"

Red felt his throat tightening. "They're … they're…"

"FLAME IT OUT!"

"They're not real!" he blurted.

"Not *real*? I don't understand."

Red took a deep breath. "I think they're undragons, Dag."

An awful silence fell. No one moved. No one even breathed. Lou felt the shock of it too.

"Are you sure? How do you know?"

"Because they signalled me—"

"What? You mean *the* signal?" asked Perilous in horror.

Red nodded. "Can't they be re-dragoned?"

Rampant turned to him. "Didn't they teach you anything at school? There's no way! Once a dragon's fire is out, it's out. That's why we never let it happen." He turned to Lou, eyes blazing. "That's why we agreed to come to this stinking place – the only reason!"

"And if they're undragoned," Red added, "and kept behind walls, the uprights can make them do things. They can control them."

There was another pause.

"So ... they're prisoners," whispered Lou.

"You mean, like you said you felt on your island?" Lou nodded.

"So, they..." Red swallowed. *"Can't get out?"*

"WHAT?" bellowed Rampant furiously. "IT'S AN OUTRAGE AND I WON'T STAND FOR IT!" He turned his head and shot out a huge fire-stream that exploded in a ball of flame. "We'll rescue them – we MUST! It's our dragon duty!"

"Yes," agreed Perilous. "Ferocity, take us to them." She reached out her forepaws to pick Lou up.

"No, not this time; I'll just slow you down," Lou said. She gave Red what he now knew was a brave *smile*. "Don't worry about me. I'll wait for you here."

"She's right, Perilous," said Rampant. He turned to the little upright and said firmly, "Don't go anywhere. We'll be back."

Moments later, the three dragons were standing in a row. Red looked over his shoulder at his friend. There she was, left behind, alone, with rain in her eyes.

"Prepare for take-off!" ordered Rampant.

As their wings began to beat, Lou, gripped suddenly by fear, called out, *"When shall we three meet again? In thunder, lightning, or in rain?"* Then, even louder: "Come back for me, Red! Promise you'll come back!"

Red turned to look at her. "Dragons always come back!" he shouted over the sound of beating wings.

Then they had lift-off. Next time they looked down, they could see Lou staring up at them, one hand raised in a longing wave. As Red wheeled around and headed for the place where he'd seen the undragons, an extraordinary think came to him: was it possible that a dragon could be friends with an upright – truly friends? If it were possible – *if* – then it might mean something really important.

Maybe something much bigger.

CHAPTER 32

Lou had wanted to stay and wait for the dragons' return, but something stopped her, a fear perhaps that they wouldn't keep their word, or worse – that they might not *make* it back. Those strange people, who'd appeared without warning and disappeared just as quickly at the sight of the full-growns, had brandished weapons that had struck dread into her heart.

She knew she had to do something to stop them from using them. She had to explain that the dragons were friendly. Despite herself, she'd begun to care deeply about the fate of the three dragons; they were also still, she presumed, her only way home. Shortly after they'd flown away across the trees, Lou ran in the other direction until, hungry and tired, she could run no more. Then she walked.

Soon she reached the first of the strange buildings – the beginning of the skyscraper people's village. But it wasn't a village like the one she'd grown up in. It reminded her of places she'd read about called *towns*. She and her father had imagined them together, and he'd told her stories of great bustling places, before the rise of dragons, filled with life and excitement and with every incredible thing humankind had ever made. And here, possibly, stood the remains of just such a place. That she might now see it was hard to believe.

The streets were wide and solidly paved, not narrow and mud-packed like at home, and they were crowded with people. They too were different. Their clothes amazed her. They weren't like the simple garments her people wore. They were elaborate and beautiful. The women's tunics were covered with patterns that Lou wanted to touch. Not painted on, but stitched, with bright stones and shells mixed in – far beyond what was needed to hold the pieces of cloth together. The men wore different things but also brightly coloured. Lou looked down at her plain homespun tunic over baggy trousers and felt a little embarrassed.

The dwellings lining the streets were very tall compared with the ones she knew, and those near by had several houses built on top of each other. At the base of them were markets with food for sale –

luscious-looking fruits, the likes of which she'd never seen before. Hunger gnawed at her the moment she set eyes on them. She knew it was wrong to steal but she couldn't help it. Her hand reached out by itself and closed around something red and soft. Before she could bring it to her watering mouth, someone seized her wrist.

"Stop! Thief!"

Lou wrenched herself free and bolted.

She didn't know if she was being chased, but she quickly turned a corner and soon got lost in the crowd. Eventually, having run to the point of exhaustion, she found a wall and slumped against it, gasping for breath. Her eyes fell on something on her hand – a red liquid creeping over her fingers…

Blood?

She blinked, then realized: that's not blood – it's juice!

There, at her feet, was the fruit she'd stolen. She snatched it up and took a bite, savouring the sweetness and letting the delicious juice fill her with energy. As she wiped her lips, she heard something: a rumbling, faint at first, but quickly getting louder. Moments later, around the corner came a cart full of goods driven by a man and pulled—

By a dragon!

It was green like Perilous, but shaped differently: longer, thinner, less ... what? Dignified? Unlike Red and his parents, this one ran on all fours, and wore a harness, its wings tied to its sides, its jaws bound shut. Lou, as she stared, couldn't help thinking of her own dragons – and how they might react to such treatment. It didn't bear thinking about! And she knew there'd been a time, not long ago, when such a sight might have

given her little cause for concern – satisfaction, even.
But now, after all she'd been through – after everything
she'd learned – the sight of a dragon at the mercy of
a human shook her to the core.

As it passed her, she felt suddenly light-headed, then
the ground rushed up to meet her.

When Lou woke up, she was lying on something
soft, in a room with patterns on the walls. There
were people standing around her – skyscraper
people. A kind hand stroked her face, and then came
a woman's heavily accented voice.

"Where ye from, lassie?"

Lou shook her head wearily. "A village. I'm from
a village ... on an island called Haven."

The woman turned to the others, frowning. Then
she turned back. "Where's yer island? Near here?"

"No, it's far away."

"Far away?" The others looked at one another
incredulously. "Then where's yer boat?" the woman
asked.

"We didn't come by boat. My dragons brought me."

The word *dragons* seemed to hit the woman like

a mallet. The whole room went silent. Lou gazed
at the stunned faces staring back at her. Suddenly
a man pushed his way to her bedside. She recognized
him from the first meeting: the one called Monolo.

"How did yer dragons get 'ere?" he said, eyes fixed
on her.

"They flew—"

There were gasps, disbelieving faces, and
fearful whisperings. Then an old woman – the one
who'd grabbed Monolo when the full-growns had
charged – appeared. She took Lou's smooth hand in
her wrinkled one.

"Are ye saying the wee red dragon's nae the only
one that can fly?"

Lou nodded.

Monolo stared at her for a moment, then at the old
woman, then at the others. There was more whispering,
shaking of heads, a growing unease. He bent over Lou,
his voice taking on a more urgent tone.

"Tell me – where're yer dragons now?"

The kindness Lou had felt when she first opened
her eyes, like the light in the room, seemed now to
be fading. The muttering became much louder and
more threatening. She ached for her dragons. Those

powerful bodies that had once instilled such dread now seemed to offer only comfort and protection. If only it wasn't from people.

Another voice cut in; a younger man's. "The girl's lyin'."

"What? I'm not! I'm not lying!"

Lou struggled to sit up, and grew dizzy again. Something inside felt worse than loneliness and confusion. It was hunger. But there was no sympathy in the eyes of the strangers now, nor were they interested in her protests or her empty belly.

They rushed out of the room, calling to one another to find these dragons at all costs. Soon they had all gone. Only Monolo remained.

"Where're yer dragons?" he demanded fiercely. "Tell me!"

"I don't know; they flew off somewhere…"

The man leaned closer – so close she could feel his hot breath on her face.

"Tell me," he said urgently. "Tell me or I'll mek ye wish ye had!"

CHAPTER 33

The three dragons had arrived at the walled-in place but they were having trouble communicating because these new dragons didn't seem to speak. Red did the best he could by using tail-signals, which all dragons know, and those behind the walls signalled back. In that way Red grasped at least part of what they were saying.

"It's what you thought, Dag," he said, as the undragons crowded the barrier, thrusting their heads over it to sniff and nuzzle the newcomers. "They can't fly so they can't get out. The uprights built the walls too high." There was a pause for more signalling. "And they do what the skyscraper peepuls tell them…"

"Or what?" snarled Rampant, feeling his chest-fire heating up.

"They don't feed them."

"What exactly do the uprights tell them to do?"

asked Perilous, who was politely nuzzling one of the female undragons while her pair knocked horns with some of the males crowding and jostling at the wall. These new dragons didn't seem to understand this greeting and backed away in alarm.

"They work," said Red.

"Work?"

"Yes. I think they lift and … and drag things … and the peepuls ride the mumbos."

"*Ride* them? What for?" asked Perilous, horrified.

Red consulted one of the younger ones. "If other peepuls come – bad peepuls – the dragons have to chase them away."

Rampant drew back his head in shock. "You mean to tell me that the uprights use them for *fighting*? They defend uprights – from what? Enemy uprights?" Red nodded. "So they're an upright *defence force*? Wait till I show them a *dragon* attack force!"

The black dragon began swiping at the wall with his snout, tearing great chunks out of it. Perilous looked on, trying to control the sudden violent impulse welling up inside her. But she couldn't do it.

"They're *still* fighting," she growled. "After all this time. After everything that's happened! Haven't they learned ANYTHING?" She joined her pair, bashing the stone barrier with her front paws. The undragons reeled back.

"Mag! Dag! Stop! You're scaring them!" cried Red. He blew white smoke to calm the undragons, but this only seemed to bewilder them. "What if they don't *want* to attack?"

Rampant paused his work of destruction. "Why wouldn't they? You think they want to stay shut in here – captives until life-over?"

Red saw that the undragons were now huddled in groups, mumbling and snorting, and making no attempt to escape. He'd seen other animals do the same back home – horn-runners and such – after his parents chased them and herded them into groups, huddled and shaking, waiting for life-over. There was something undignified about a dragon behaving the same way.

"Look at them, Dag. They don't want to fight. They don't want to do anything. Maybe they like it here."

"You think any self-respecting dragon would prefer being captive to being free?"

"They're not self-respecting dragons, though, are they?" put in his pair. "They're undragons, remember?"

"What are we going to do, Dag?"

For a moment, Rampant stood still: neck erect, horns tilted forward at a menacing angle. He gave a dismissive huff of smoke.

"We have a mission," he said. "We've come here for coal. And we're not leaving without it."

"What about your dragon duty?" said Red.

"My duty is to the Council. Nothing more. Now ask them, son. You ask them where the uprights keep the coal."

Red turned to the undragons and signalled the word *coal*. As soon as he did, their drooping ears perked up. He turned back to his dag.

"They know where it is, lots of it. We've come to the right place!"

Perhaps their mission could succeed after all. They'd come in search of coal and here it was. If they could only get their paws on it. But for some reason, the good feeling that flickered through their think-spaces was quickly extinguished by something deeper and more important. A new mission had emerged, one they'd never expected, but one which their dragonsense urged them not to ignore.

Rampant growled deep in his throat. "These undragons *can* fight. They've already told us as much. What we need to do now is convince them to fight for *themselves*."

He retreated, threw his head back, opened his throat and gave vent to a great, challenging ROOAAARRRR. Fire leaped out of his throat. The undragons stood perfectly still until first one, then another, and another, and finally all of them, put their heads back, opened their throats as Rampant had, and let out—

A smokeless bellow?

The sound, though not as impressive as a full-dragon's, was still fierce and challenging. Several of them rose on their back legs and slashed at the air with their claws. Tails came up, and the signals they gave now were anything but wretched and defeated.

Red, watching, felt something blazing up inside him, ancient and irresistible.

There was a word for that, too.

Rage.

CHAPTER 34

Not far away, Lou sat alone in the room where she'd awoken, wondering what to do. The skyscraper people's interest had quickly shifted from her to the dragons. If she'd felt hunger before, now it was like a stabbing pain in the pit of her stomach. She had to find food somehow! But where?

In through the open door crept two children: a boy and a girl who looked a bit younger than her. When the girl saw Lou, she stared shyly at her for a moment, then tentatively held something out. An apple! Lou snatched it and took a giant bite, closing her eyes and relishing the juicy crunch.

"Thank you!" she said finally, when she remembered her manners.

The boy put out his hand. "Al' right? My name's Gedeon," he said. Lou was too busy chomping on the apple to respond. The boy asked, "What's yers?"

"I'm Lou," she managed through the last mouthful.

"Lou," the girl repeated, as if enjoying the sound. "I'm Elie."

"Hi, Elie," mumbled Lou, swallowing the last of the apple. "You don't have anything else to eat, do you?"

The boy produced another piece of fruit, one Lou didn't recognize. It was round like the apple, but a different colour.

"What's that?" Lou asked.

"Tha's an orange," Elie told her. Lou touched its bright dimpled surface before biting into it.

"Ha! Yer have to peel it afore ye eat it!"

Gedeon snatched the fruit from her and began to peel it, then he split it open and handed it back. Lou looked at it quizzically, then took a bite.

"Delicious!" she exclaimed, wiping her mouth. "We don't have these at home."

There were faint sounds from outside the room. The children stiffened.

"Come wi' us!" whispered Elie, and she took Lou's hand. "Quick!"

She pulled Lou off the bed and led her to the door. Gedeon opened it a crack and listened, then he beckoned to them both.

299

"C'mon! But you'll have to be quiet."

As the three children crept through the house, Lou couldn't help noticing how beautiful it was, full of interesting objects. The walls weren't wooden, like at home, but made of something smooth and strong and cool to the touch. The roof wasn't thatched with reeds or straw, but made of pieces of flat grey stone, and there were window holes of different shapes, not square like in her house. And they were filled with something.

"I know what this is!" she said excitedly. "Glass!"

Gedeon and Elie stared at her for a moment, then looked at each other, breaking into giggles.

"I've seen pictures in books." Lou reached out and touched the clear material. "I can't believe you have glass. But why isn't it coloured?"

Oh, where were her dragons? She couldn't wait to tell them about it – Red especially. About all the clever, wonderful things she'd seen. Even Rampant might be impressed.

"C'mon!" urged Elie, grabbing Lou's hand again and pulling her on. "If yer stay here ye'll be in danger."

The skyscrapers, Lou soon discovered, were not for living in – not the higher parts at least. They were far too damaged. But lower down they were sturdy and beautiful, covered with coloured stones stuck in patterns. It was the same on the roofs and the paths and the firm dry roads. These people loved art – that was obvious – and they were good at it, too.

Another plentiful thing they had here was people. They were everywhere, walking, bustling about the shops, and riding in carts pulled by dragons.

It was good that Gedeon and Elie were with her, or she might have been knocked down by one of these. Lou was filled with an unsettling mixture of shame and pride: shame that people could capture dragons and force them to work and fight for them; pride that they could create such unbelievable things.

As they rounded a corner, Lou was amazed to see the structure that loomed up ahead – not as tall as a skyscraper, but better preserved, and even more decorated. She stopped to look. It had rounded sides and a roof like an upside-down bowl, and it was huge. Sticking out of the top was a pole with symbols on it. The windows weren't clear, like the ones in the houses, but seemed painted. Here was the coloured glass that she'd seen in pictures.

"What *is* this place?" Lou asked in wonder.

"This? Eh, 'tis our God place."

There was something different about the way Gedeon said it, a tone she hadn't heard before, more quiet, more solemn. Whatever this place was, it held great meaning for him, she could tell.

"Can we go in?"

"Not now," he told her. "We need to get ye away. Ye've brought flyin' dragons, and that's forbidden."

They drew her onward but Lou kept looking back at the building, the upside-down bowl glinting in the sun.

"Is it true wha' they say?" said the girl. "Yer dragons don't work?"

"All I know is, they don't work for *me*," Lou replied. "They're my friends."

The skyscraper children stopped and looked at each other. Then Gedeon turned to Lou, his expression betraying suspicion.

"Yer *muckers*? Wi' dragons?"

Lou nodded. The boy didn't say anything; he just stared at her. The girl too. Lou felt uneasy, the way she had when the mood had changed among the adults questioning her in the house – when the friendliness had faded.

"We weren't friends – er, muckers – at first, obviously," she explained. "My people hate dragons. I hated them too. But that was before I met any. Then I spoke to them and got to know them."

"Are ye saying yer dragons can talk?" Gedeon flashed his sister another puzzled look. He clearly didn't believe a word he was hearing.

"Honestly, Red can't stop talking! He loves words –

his favourite's *imagination* – and he's always learning new ones; he's clever like that."

"You call 'im Red? You know a *red* dragon?"

"Whoa!" shouted Elie and she clapped her hands together in excitement. The boy and girl began to sing.

"When th' Red Red Dragon comes out o' the sea, what a day that will be fer him and fer me..."

A loud noise broke into their conversation – a crashing, thunderous roaring. They all looked round, then up and—

"There they are!" shouted Lou.

She pointed at three shapes looking, to eyes that had never seen such a thing before, like giant birds blotting out the sun, great wings outstretched, bodies of armoured scales, necks craned purposefully before them. Her companions' eyes were fixed on the sight, their feet rooted, trying to take it all in.

Lou's three dragons flew slowly, deliberately, towards them. But the closer they got, the clearer it became: they weren't the ones making all the noise. That terrible roaring sound wasn't coming from the air.

It was coming from the ground.

CHAPTER 35

The children couldn't see what was making the sound because of the buildings in the way, but suddenly Gedeon seemed to understand, and the knowledge clearly filled his heart with dread.

"Our dragons! They must've escaped!"

He and Elie tore off, leaving Lou standing there alone. Seconds later, Gedeon was back, grabbing Lou by the wrist and pulling her after him, back to the God place. He pushed her in through the double doors and tumbled in after, Elie close behind. Then he slammed the doors.

Lou had a moment to take in the inside of the building. It was huge and solid and beautiful beyond words – even Shakespeare's. There were glass windows of many colours. The sun pierced through in shafts, flinging patterns all over the smooth, shiny floor. The roof was far above them. The ceiling had elaborate pictures painted on, showing, among other things, Lou's favourite: angels. But the most wonderful thing was the books, rows and rows of them, ranged on long shelves. And there were statues, too, carved from wood or moulded from clay but much larger and more detailed than anything her father had ever made.

"Where did you get all these?" Lou gasped.

Gedeon and Elie didn't answer. Instead they pulled her to a big table at the far end, and pushed her under it. The three of them crouched there, in semi-darkness, hidden behind a cloth that hung down all around the table.

"We're safe here," said the girl in a tiny voice. "God'll mek sure."

"Who is God?" asked Lou.

The boy looked at her blankly for a moment. Then he said, "He's al' around."

Before he could say any more, there was an uprush of noise from outside, a crashing and roaring that was loud despite the thick walls. Lou felt Gedeon and Elie stiffen beside her. The sound grew louder and louder, until the books on the shelves began to tremble and shake. Elie whimpered, pressing her hands to her ears.

Peering out from under the cloth, Lou caught

a movement outside one the windows, blotting out the light. Elie screamed. Gedeon grabbed her and clapped his hand over her mouth. The girl stared wildly over his fingers, breathing in muffled gasps.

Gedeon whispered to Lou in terror, "They've come ter eat us!"

"No, no, dragons aren't like that any more! Look, I'll prove it."

Gedeon's hand snapped out to grab her, but too late – she'd already scrambled out from under the table and was on her feet, running the length of the God place to the big doors at the end. She swung them open, then fell backwards before the terrifying sight that met her eyes.

Everywhere she looked were dragons!

Bounding along the road, clambering onto the low houses and up the walls of the higher ones, smashing things, tearing them down, flapping their wings and waving their tails. Now the same incredible strength that the uprights had harnessed to do their bidding was being used against them, unleashed for destruction, all accompanied by those ear-shattering sounds that pierced the air and made the earth shake.

Suddenly a massive green undragon sprang in front

of Lou and lowered its head to sniff her. She had no time to think. She kicked wildly against its mighty head, trying to push it away. But it was useless. The creature stretched its giant maw wide enough to chomp down and make mincemeat of her.

Something swooped and grabbed her under her arms, lifting her high in the air. She had no breath to scream. Then came a familiar voice, and with it, a surge of relief.

"It's all right, Lou! It's me! It's Red!"

Red soared higher and higher, then banked. Next thing Lou knew, they were coming in to land, not on the ground but far

above it, on the square top of a vast skyscraper – the one that still stood tall. Red put Lou gently down.

Far below they could

see turmoil in the streets, but not the scene of carnage she'd feared. The skyscraper people were converging on the God place with the dragons surging after them.

"Look!" Lou shouted. "They're going into the God place! They must think it's safe!"

"They're probably right – dragons don't usually go into upright live-places. These ones have probably been living outside since the Great Ridding."

We believed the Great Ridding got rid of uprights, Red thought. Yet here they still are. And here *we* still are. We've never got rid of each other. A strange think came creeping into his think-space.

"Where are your mag and dag?" Lou asked.

"Down there somewhere, with the others."

Lou scanned the scene and thought she could make out Rampant's flailing wings and claws, Perilous a little way behind.

Lou turned to face Red. "You have to *do* something! The dragons are out of control."

"What can *I* do?"

"Something! I mean, you're the Red Dragon, the one in the song!"

"Why d'you keep saying that?"

"Because it's true!"

"No, it isn't! Anyway, there must be other red dragons."

Lou looked down. "No. You're the only one."

All of a sudden Red felt afraid. Not of being so high up, and not of the chaos that seemed to be raging below. He was afraid of what she expected of him – what everyone seemed to expect from him. Come on! he thought. I'm just an ordinary mumbo – red, yes; a prize-winning flyer, that too – but *not* the one everyone's been waiting for; *not* the one who can cause everything to be all right again.

There was a long pause, then Red lifted his head. "Why me, Lou? Why's it *always* me?"

She took his forepaws in her hands. "*To be, or not to be; that is the question*," she said. "None of us can change the question, Red. But maybe you can change the answer."

A sudden gust of wind whipped over the roof, so strong it almost knocked Lou off her feet. As Red steadied her, he suddenly froze, sniffing the air, nostrils sucking in a new smell.

Coal! He took a moment to savour the wonderful, chest-fire-lighting scent. Then he turned to Lou, invigorated. "It doesn't matter," he said.

"What doesn't?"

"If I'm the one in the song or not." He stared at her, wide-eyed with hope. "It doesn't take a special colour to change the answer. It takes a special *think-space*. And I can't believe I'm the only one with that."

Lou gazed at him admiringly and began to sing. *"When the Red Red Dragon comes over the hill, I know he will come to heal and not kill!"*

Red spread his wings purposefully. "Now, we have to cause griffilin."

"Griffilin? But – you said that was the impossible think. What does it even mean?"

"I *said* it was. But look at us now – we're friends – a dragon and an upright – actually friends! I'd never have believed it. But now I know: things are only impossible until someone does them."

She smiled at her clever red dragon, then swiftly climbed onto his back, flattening his fins. They stood on the edge of the great building that uprights in the Old Time had made. Suddenly Red, with claws on the edge, hesitated.

"What's wrong?" she whispered.

"I'm afraid again."

"Don't be. You're safe with me."

Red looked down. The ground seemed to pull away from him.

"Say those words," he said, "the ones you said before to make me brave!"

"You mean 'Angels and ministers'?" Red nodded. Lou took a deep breath and then shouted, *"Angels and ministers of grace – DEFEND US!"*

Her words soared, just as Red, revived, suddenly felt he could soar. He rustled his wings and spread them.

"And make us strong and clever!" he roared, his voice rising above the sounds of flight and the din below. "Enough to cause GRIFFILIN!"

Lou gripped with her knees, clutched his topmost fin until her knuckles whitened, and closed her eyes tight as he launched off the edge.

What could griffilin be? Suddenly, in this breath-stopping moment, she knew.

It meant something there'd never been, not in the Old Time or now, between her kind and Red's. Lou had a word for it too. A beautiful word that Shakespeare used when Romeo's friend was trying to stop him fighting: *I do but keep the peace…*

Yes. That must be it.

Griffilin meant *peace*.

CHAPTER 36

Rampant and Perilous were standing in front of the doors of the God place. The skyscraper peepuls were crammed inside.

All around, the newly freed undragons were wreathing their necks, flapping their unusable wings, and making snarling, grunting noises – half threatening, half baffled. Rampant, determined to get their attention, took off and hovered above them. His wings made loud clapping sounds and his roaring voice rose above the general din.

"UNDRAGONS! You've been turned into captives: set to work and made ashamed! You've forgotten – uprights *made* you forget – who you are. *What* you are!" He looked down at them. "Our scales are strong! Our claws are sharp! Our fire is hot! Soon you'll make homes of their live-places, fuel of their coal, and food of THEM—"

"COOKED!" added Perilous as she rose beside him.

"GET READY TO RIP-BURN-KILL!"

United, the two dragons blew out long flames and turned in the air towards the built-thing into which the uprights had been herded. But then came something incredible – something neither of them expected: a great bellow of protest from the undragons. Tails came erect, and, as one, they signalled: *NOOOO!*

It was as if the wind went out of the full-growns' wings, and they dropped to the ground. At that moment, Red and Lou landed beside them. Rampant stared at his son in amazement.

"Ferocity Bychaheadoff! Where in Flame's name have you been?"

"Up there!" Red pointed to the skyscraper roof with his tail.

"You should've been down here with us!"

"I thought one of the undragons was trying to attack Lou. I had to save her, Dag."

Rampant cast his eyes down on the little upright and gave a grunt. "Well, you're back now." He nodded towards the crowd of agitated undragons. "I think you were right about this lot – they won't fight."

Red looked at them, trying to make sense of their

urgent signals. "They're saying they don't want to hurt the uprights."

"Why not? Don't they want to be free?"

Red plunged into the mass of undragons. They huddled around him, bellowing, trying to be understood. Red turned to his parents.

"They signal that they've lived with uprights. They know they have the Power of the Hand. They can do things – things we can't."

"What are you saying?" asked Rampant dangerously. "That uprights are better than dragons?"

"It's not about who's better, or which of us is cleverer or stronger, Dag. What matters is that we could be cleverer and stronger – together."

"*Together?*" Rampant spluttered, as if he'd champed on a rotten fur-hopper and had to spit it out in disgust.

"It's a lot better than killing one another," Lou retorted.

There was a pause while Rampant took this in. Or at least tried to.

"But that would mean … sharing the mainland…"

"Right, Dag. The mainland, the land-lumps – I mean *islands*. Everywhere."

As Rampant stood there, hearing his son's words,

he felt something – something far more powerful than he'd ever known, tearing at all he knew; at everything he believed.

Dragons and uprights *together*? Impossible! Unthinkable!

The think was so terrifying, so utterly unacceptable, that the huge black dragon was momentarily silenced.

"Dag?"

When Rampant finally spoke, his voice had changed: it was deeper, more of a growl.

"There's coal here. Plenty of it. These others – they didn't need to be undragoned. The uprights denied them! If they hadn't, they'd have been driven out of this place – just like they were in the Great Ridding."

"And if that had happened, Dag, things would've just gone back to the way they used to be in the Old Time. There'd have been fighting and rip-burn-killing and—"

"YES! And dragons would've won, as dragons always do!" Rampant stretched himself to full height and puffed out his chest. "That's the way things should be, isn't it?"

Red stared at his dag. He saw an unfamiliar glint of coldness in his gaze. He was talking about something that had been passed down from dragon to mumbo over many hatchings: fixed, unthinking, immovable. And suddenly Red knew.

That's what I must do! I must CHANGE it!

"Dag, listen to me! What if rip-burn-killing *isn't* the way it should be? What if dragons and uprights are meant to help each other: uprights with their hands, and dragons with—"

"What? Our strength? Working and fighting when we're told to?"

"No! Dag, listen." Then it came, bright as a flare in his think-space. "We can teach them to talk-not-quarrel. We can teach them decency not violence."

"Clever dragons!" Lou exclaimed. She was still on Red's back, lying low behind his neck. But now she raised her head. "If people stopped fighting, there'd be more of us. I mean – when was the last time you heard of a dragon killing another *dragon*?"

"NEVER!" the full-growns answered together.

"Exactly," said Lou. "Then that's what dragons can do: they can teach us how to live peacefully."

But Rampant would not be swayed. "Among all your upright words, have you one for someone who lives in their think-space and not in the real world?"

He was looking at Ferocity now.

"Yes. A *dreamer*. But Red's not the only one."

"I'm sick and tired of all your words. Words are for uprights. DOs are for Dragons! And what we have to DO right now is rid this place of uprights – the ones who undragoned our kind."

Rampant breathed white-hot flame towards the God place. Red hardly felt Lou tug on his fins as she slid down off his back. He had talked-not-quarrelled, but no agreement had come.

His parents were moving in.

And the undragons, even the ones who had hesitated before, pressed forward now, led by these newcomers who could fly and breathe fire. Red backed off as the flames shot towards the doors of the God place.

Then a shrill voice behind him cut through the din.

"If you burn them, you'll have to burn me first!"

CHAPTER 37

Lou had thrown herself against the doors of the God place. Now she stood braced, arms outstretched, barring the way.

"Tell her to move, son!" bellowed Rampant.

Lou stood firm. "*Think* for a second, will you!" she yelled above the menacing grunts of the undragons. "How will you make your dragons *real* again without the help of these people? You can't! We all have to talk!"

"I told you," roared Red's dag. "The time for talking is OVER."

"Wait!" said Perilous. "Think of the mission. We need coal. *Their* coal. If we start fighting, they'll never give it to us – and this whole journey will have been for nothing."

Rampant smacked the ground with his tail and clacked his wings.

"All right," he grunted reluctantly. "Let's talk. But if they don't agree – WE'LL END THEM!"

There was a pause, then Lou turned and banged on the doors with both fists.

"Let me in!" she shouted. "The dragons want to talk!"

There was no reply.

"See!" thundered Rampant. "It's useless! Uprights never listen."

"They're afraid," Lou replied.

"THEY SHOULD BE!" Rampant roared, and he turned to the other dragons. "SMASH IT IN!"

"No, Dag, NO!"

It was Red. He threw his shoulder against one of the doors and it fell inwards. Lou ducked straight under his chest and now she could see the people crammed inside, huddled as far from the entrance as possible, Gedeon and Elie among them, white-faced. Monolo was there too, trying to shield the two children – perhaps he was their dad?

Every face wore a look of terror.

Lou ran to the table where she'd hidden before and climbed onto it, signalling for calm.

"It's all right! Don't be afraid! They're not going to hurt you!"

The people exchanged terrified looks and began to whisper. Lou glanced at Red, halfway through the door, but he stayed where he was, not wanting to make things worse by coming in. She turned back to the people.

"You and your dragons have lived together all this time. Can you imagine life without them?" She paused for a moment. "You need them. And they need you. Come on – who agrees?"

At first there was only silence. Then a murmuring, and slowly, first one hand then another went up. Lou continued.

"What would you do to prove to them you could live together – that you're not afraid of them? Would you free them and help them to be full-dragons?" Bewildered expressions greeted this. "Could you *trust* them? Oh, if only you could trust them, and they could trust *you*!"

Outside the God place, the low, continuous growling had quieted. The only voice now was Red's, coming through the broken door.

"Keep talking, Lou," he urged. "Dag was wrong. Uprights *can* listen!"

In the silence Lou wracked her brain for words – words to persuade; words to inspire; words to bring dragons and uprights towards peace. But before she could say anything, Monolo came forward. He spoke quietly.

"There's somethin' I think ye should see. All o' you."

He walked behind the table with the white cloth, where the three children had hidden. In the wall behind it, there was a door. He took a key from his pocket and unlocked it. He reached inside and lifted out something large and heavy, putting it on the table in full view of everyone.

"What's going on in there?" bellowed Rampant impatiently.

The uprights inside leaned forward to see better, staring at it wide-eyed, before the ones in the front stepped back in amazement.

Lou couldn't contain herself. "Oh, look! Look!" she cried.

It was a beautifully carved wooden statue of a woman clasping something in her arms. A baby?

But it wasn't. Awestruck, Lou let her fingers play over its perfectly honed smoothness.

First those in front, and then the ones behind, by craning their necks, saw what it was. They couldn't believe their eyes.

"She's holding a baby dragon as if it were *her* baby!"

exclaimed Lou. She turned to the others. "This can't have really happened – it must just be the artist's dream. His impossible think."

Monolo nodded. "I admit I kept this from ye all; I had to, because our forefathers wanted dragons ter work fer us. But I was wrong. We were all wrong."

"It doesn't have to be an impossible dream," said Lou. "The dragons have a word: *griffilin*. I think it means peace. Don't you see? It's a sign."

A new think swept into Red's think-space. He withdrew his head and spoke to his dag and mag outside.

"There's something here you have to see: something that shows dragons and uprights can get along."

"Nonsense!" protested his dag.

"How can it be nonsense when I get along with an upright and she gets along with me? And you get along with her too, Dag; don't say you don't."

If Rampant had been honest with himself, he might have acknowledged the feeling of affection for the little upright that had crept over all of them during the course of their mission. But this niggling feeling got in the way of good dragonsense.

"You two can get along as much as you like," Rampant huffed. "What matters now is how to re-dragon these others!"

The sight of all the books in the God place suddenly gave Red a think.

"Dag! The Block of Knowledge the Council gave you – have you still got it?"

Rampant stuck his snout in his pouch. It was still there. It had caused some discomfort at first, but in the end he'd almost forgotten he still carried it.

"What about it?"

"The Council gave it to you for a reason. Now I think I know what it might be."

"Well?"

"They gave it to you because it can *talk*. Maybe the Council wanted us to use it – to talk some dragonsense into the uprights."

Red moved out of the way. Moments later, the other door, already hanging precariously on its hinges, crashed inward, and Rampant's bulk burst through. The force of his entrance made him fall flat on his snout. The people inside shrank back, Gedeon and Elie among them, but Lou beckoned the boy over to where the black dragon was wedged in the doorway, twisting and writhing, while he tried to reach his pouch.

"I can't do it; I'm stuck…"

Lou could see it was true: Rampant's belly, together with his pouch, were pressed to the floor, and his haunches were pinned in the doorway.

"Hang on!" she shouted. By lying flat, she managed to squeeze under his raised chest, and, with some effort, reach into his pouch. But something stopped her – the memory of Red's vehement reaction on the beach. Cautiously she asked, "Do you mind if I reach into—?"

"Just this once," Rampant grunted.

"What can I do?" asked Gedeon.

"The book's in here," gasped Lou. "I can feel it. If you can just help me…"

Gedeon hesitated. Putting his hand into the soft pouch would take all his courage. Then he nodded. Joining Lou on the floor, he squirmed his free arm in. Yes! It was there all right, the edge of the book…

"If we can just grab hold of it, we should be able to pull it out," urged Lou.

They gripped the hard object, but Rampant's bulk was pinning it to the floor.

"Rampant," said Lou. "You'll have to try to lift yourself up a bit."

The black dragon groaned and tried to do as he was asked, but despite his great strength, the door frame held him fast. Lou and Gedeon pulled, fingers slipping on the cover of the book. Then suddenly Perilous – still outside – put her snout under her pair and gave him a sharp nip on his hindquarters. He let out a startled snarl and jerked upward. As he did, the door frame cracked against his back. Finally, and with one last effort, Lou and Gedeon could just manage – by holding it between them – to drag the book out and wriggle backwards with it on the smooth patterned floor.

When they got to their feet, Elie was waiting for them, arms outstretched, ready to help carry the heavy book. "Well done!" she cried.

But before they could do anything with it, Monolo was at their side.

"Lemme see that," he said, taking it carefully from them. He carried it over to a beautifully decorated stand in the centre of the floor and mounted a platform behind it. Lou, Gedeon and Elie jumped up beside him, while the other people crowded round.

As Monolo opened the book, the children could see it was filled with pictures – wonderful colourful ones, mainly of animals. The man turned the pages, slowly and reverently. Then Lou gave a sudden gasp. She pointed.

"Look! Dragons!"

Monolo peered closer. "Aye..."

"What's that place?" Elie whispered.

Gedeon pointed to a picture of two dragons. Behind them were hills covered in lush greenery.

"D'ye know where this is?" the boy asked.

"Wherever it *was*," Lou said grimly, "nothing's that green any more. Must've been before the world got hot."

Rampant, still trying to back out of the doorway, made a growling interruption.

"Who cares about the flaming pic-turs! Does it say anything about re-dragoning undragons?"

"Go on, lassie. Ye read it," said Monolo, and he moved so that Lou could take his place in front of the book.

Something caught her eye. "*Diagrams*," she whispered under her breath. She looked up at Rampant. "This book's got diagrams!"

"What on this charred earth are *di-a-grams*?" growled Rampant.

"They're pictures, sort of, like smoke signals, telling you what to do."

The diagram Lou was looking at showed a dragon, a young one, like Red. It was blowing flames into the open mouth of another, a full-grown. Below it another diagram showed the inside of a dragon's chest-fire with a flame lighting it.

"I think I've found it!" Lou cried. "I think I've found how to relight their chest-fire. What we need now is a dragon, a young one…"

All eyes turned to Red, still standing by the doorway.

"Why are you all looking at *me*?" he asked.

CHAPTER 38

Some lights and darks and several big heads-togethers later, a plan was hatched. The three dragons and Lou, along with the undragons, made their way to the large open space just outside the town. There they saw great glistening heaps of coal that had been specially brought. The dragons gazed at it hungrily.

"There's enough there to fill every dragon's pouch over and over again," marvelled Perilous.

But Rampant didn't answer. He was doing something he'd never done before. He was thinking *ahead* – to how proud the Council would be of him if he managed to get this lot home.

As for the uprights, who were following some distance behind, they were not so much excited as nervous, even frightened. After all, this coal, it now seemed, would be used to turn their tame, obedient dragons into ... what? Full-grown, fighting, fire-

breathing flying ones. And: what might these real
dragons do to those who'd imprisoned them and made
them work so hard?

The coal-crunching feast began. The undragons, born
in captivity, had never eaten coal before, and at first it
tasted so strange that some of them spat it out.

"It's shameful!" Rampant whispered to his pair.
"You'd think they were being asked to eat something
rotten!"

"Come on, Rampant; coal's an acquired taste, you
know that. Back-think to your first time."

"What about it? I took it like a dragon – down in
one gulp! Just like our son when it was his turn."

"That's not what I heard. Your mag told me you were
sick as a furry-barker when you tried your first piece."

"Don't listen to her!" he retorted. "She thinks
uprights don't exist, remember?"

The black heaps were quickly consumed, leaving
only sooty traces on the grass. Now the moment Red
had feared had come. He'd been preparing himself by
eating his fill of coal and taking deep breaths to bring
his firebox to full glow. He tried to remember some of

the words Lou had used when she needed courage, but his think-space was already too crowded.

Red and Lou had discussed with the undragons what needed to happen next, and they had signalled their agreement. Rampant now encouraged the undragons, their chests weighed down with the unfamiliar heaviness of full fire-boxes, to crouch in a long line. Perilous passed along them, breathing reassuring puffs of white smoke and urging them to open their mouths as wide as possible.

Monolo stood between Elie and Gedeon at the front of the line of uprights, all of whom hung back, fearful and fascinated. The whole town was here now, not just the ones who'd been herded into the God place. Word had got round that something amazing and possibly dangerous was about to happen.

Red looked at them. "They're afraid, aren't they," he said to Lou.

"Who can blame them?"

"There's no reason for them to be afraid."

"No *reason*? Look at your mag and dag and the other full-growns!"

Red looked. "What about them?"

"They're huge, for a start. And your parents can fly.

And look at their teeth and claws. *Scary*. Oh, and another thing in case you hadn't noticed: they breathe FIRE!"

"Only when they have to." Red gave a little snort, as close as dragons get to a chuckle, and it made him feel braver.

Taking direction from the diagrams in the book, Red started at the beginning of the line. Breathing deeply, he put his snout into the open jaws of a large brown undragon. He'd never stared down the throat of a full-grown before and he didn't like what he saw. It put an unpleasant image into his think-space: a ground-flapper's-eye view of the horrible moment just before life-over. The smell of the brown dragon's firebox seared the young dragon's nostrils.

"PHEEEW!"

He was about to snatch his snout back when he heard his dag's agitated voice behind him.

"All right, son. It's now or never."

Red hesitated. Then he drew breath and, to his own surprise, blew a thin stream of fire: not the usual sort, but blue! It hissed down the undragon's throat, and a moment later, with a muffled bang, something deep down lit up the roof of her gaping mouth. Red jumped back, shocked.

"I think it worked," he gasped. Then he shouted, "I really think it worked!"

The brown dragon shook her head violently and sneezed a vivid shower of sparks into Red's face. Then, encouraged by a new and invigorating feeling in her think-space, she rose to her full height, inhaled deeply … and blasted out her first rushing, roaring full-dragon flame.

A moment later, she spread her wings and beat the air with all her strength. Though they were weak from lack of use, she managed to lift herself half her height off the ground. The uprights fell back in alarm. Only Elie stepped forward and joined Lou in her clapping and excitement, which helped to calm the onlookers.

As Red went from one undragon to another, steadily re-dragoning them, Lou ran joyfully over to the first now-full-dragon and threw her arms round her neck. There was a collective gasp from the uprights.

"I can feel it!" Lou cried. "I can feel the new heat in its chest!"

Her voice rang out over the two groups standing facing each other. And now she was coaxing this giant armoured, almost-flying-already, fire-breathing creature across the open space to where the uprights were huddled. They shrank back nervously.

"Well?" Lou asked, her voice rising, face alight. "Aren't you going to congratulate it?"

"Her!" corrected Perilous, following closely in case of accidents.

"Yes, sorry. Go on, Perilous, you introduce *her*."

After a small amount of signalling, Perilous turned to the crowd of uprights and announced, "Please be very decent – to Deadly!" The crowd murmured uneasily. "Actually," said Perilous haughtily, "her full name, which is more appropriate now that she's a full-dragon, is Deadly Dangerous."

"Deadly Dangerous?" repeated Lou in a strained voice. "Why do dragons always have to have such scary names?"

Perilous flinched. "It came from the Old Time. When we needed to frighten peepuls away."

"But that's in the past. You don't need to frighten them now, do you? So Deadly here doesn't need to be called Deadly any more – do you?" Lou gazed up into the gentle eyes of the brown dragon. Deadly gave a snort of agreement and thumped the ground with her tail.

"Why don't you let her choose her *own* name, Mag?" Red asked.

The green dragon looked at her son – her very clever and sometimes quite annoying son.

"Very well," she said, huffing. "Ask her what she wants to call herself."

Red turned to Deadly and tail-signalled her. The brown dragon signalled enthusiastically back.

"She wants her name to be…" He looked round at his mag. "Delicious."

"*DELICIOUS?*" shouted Rampant, appearing suddenly next to his pair. "What sort of name is *that* for a dragon? Sounds more like something you'd call a fur-hopper or a ground-flapper or something else you'd crush."

"I like it," said Perilous firmly. "And since we're in a name-changing-mood, how about I change mine?"

"What?"

"From now on, I'd like to be known as…" She thought for a moment. "Precious."

Rampant looked even more appalled than before.

"If you think I'm going to call you – no, no, I can't say it – then you must be out of your FLAMING THINK-SPACE!"

CHAPTER 39

Red was now far down the line of dragons, close
to exhaustion, his firebox almost empty. Between
powerful fire-lighting gulps, he muttered under his
smoky breath, "Why me? Why does it *always* have to
be me...?"

But it was no use complaining. There was still work
to be done. Every so often he had to return to the
coal pile to replenish his firebox. Apart from that, it
was only those angels and ministers and a good bit of
dragonsense that somehow kept him going.

Finally he finished. As the last blue flame rushed
out of his throat, and the familiar bang came from
the last undragon's chest, he felt a sudden tingling
lightness in his think-space ...

... and collapsed.

Not gently or gracefully, as he might have done if
he'd considered the crowd of uprights staring at him,

but with an awkward thud. Almost immediately one of the braver uprights nearest to him in the crowd, together with the nearest dragon, rushed to help him to his feet.

"Lemme help you," said the upright, brushing the dust off Red and patting him, while the dragon nuzzled him and blew its first puff of pure white healing smoke over him.

Red stood there for a moment, trying hard not to wobble.

"Yes, yes, all right! I'm fine, *thank* you very much," he said, trying to hide his shame, straightening himself to full height in an attempt to regain his dignity.

This little scene had sent a ripple of encouragement through the rest of the crowd, and now there was movement among the uprights. They came in ones and twos, cautiously at first, then more confidently, seeing the now-full-dragons with fresh eyes.

The first to cross the space between them was Gedeon.

Red watched, impressed by this young upright's boldness. Soon he was standing right next to one of the full-dragons, a large female. She was dappled

green, with horns that curved and nostrils that
chugged the air, emitting wisps of freshly made smoke.
She stared down at him quizzically.

There was a moment of terrifying uncertainty
when everyone held their breath, but then she lowered
her head till it was level with his. He reached out
a cautious hand and touched her snout. She gave an
uncertain jolt, but he didn't draw back.

Instead he whispered something.

She lowered her snout again, and this time –
amazing to all who saw it – she nuzzled his hand,
allowing his fingers to play over her leathery features.

Then he turned round and shouted, "Th' dragon understands me; she wants to be muckers!"

There was a surge forward from both sides, and a meeting of hands and paws and skin and scales.

Red returned from his duties, limping and still aching from the effort and the fall, his wings trailing wearily. Lou ran to meet him.

"Red! Oh, Red, you did it; I knew you could!" she cried and flung her arms around him.

"I did, didn't I?" he replied, disbelievingly.

Rampant appeared beside them. "Come on, you two," he said gruffly. "Let's go somewhere private. Somewhere we can talk."

After a drink of water offered by one of the uprights, Red, with Lou perched on his back, took off and led his mag and dag to the one place he knew they could be alone: the top of the still-standing skyscraper. After they landed, Rampant stood motionless for a long time, taking in deep breaths. Then he turned to his family.

"Well?" he said wearily. "What do we do now?"

Red stared at his dag. He'd never heard him ask for

advice before. It made him uncomfortable.

Lou answered. "I'll tell you what we do now," she said. "We celebrate! Thanks to the book and the diagram and Red, everything's all right again!"

"All right? Bah! It's *far* from all right!" Rampant growled. "We've found coal, yes, and plenty of it, but how are we supposed to take it home with us?" No one answered. "What does the Council expect us to do exactly – stuff it in our pouches?" He shook his head angrily. "Everyone with their Blocks of Knowledge and their diagrams and their fancy new words! Everyone with their *feelings* and their brilliant *thinks*. And no one with answers!" He breathed out a cloud of dark smoke. "One think's certain: if we don't get going soon, it'll be too late, and our mission will have failed."

BLOCK IX
THE
JOURNEY
HOME

CHAPTER 40

On an island lost to the rest of the world in a time when people had been banished by dragons, a man stood, shaded by the leaves of a tall oak near a pebble beach. He was shaping a large piece of wood – an old tree trunk, dried out and just right for carving.

He was an artist, and he knew his craft.

With a hammer and chisel he'd struck at the wood, knocking away chunk by chunk, chip by chip, with hard, angry blows. He'd been working on it for many, many days, letting everything else in his life go hang. Nothing, it seemed, mattered more than the making of this statue. And now it was nearly finished. He'd shaped the huge, life-sized figure that was the main feature; shaped its great erect body and its half-spread wings. In its jaws was a child, face contorted, arms outstretched as if imploring rescue.

His child.

Lou. As he'd last seen her before that pitiless monster had borne her away for ever. This man had never seen a living dragon until that day on the beach when they'd visited for supplies, and that enormous beast had sprung from the cave, spewing flames, and driving them back to the sea. But he'd had a chance to observe them closely when they were on the boat home, and when the little red one had turned on the villagers, holding the people off while the big male was swooping down to snatch Lou, his only daughter.

Oh, he'd seen dragons then, filled his brain with them in all their merciless cruelty. And what he'd seen had its own power to carve – memory as solid as any pillar of weathered oak. When he imagined what must have been his daughter's end, his blood ran hot and cold and he longed for revenge.

But what was the use? She was gone. And the monsters with her.

All that was left was a hewn tribute that would stand on the shore of his island as a mark of his love for what he'd lost. And even that, he knew, nature itself would eventually destroy. Then there'd be nothing. Not even a trace.

Lou's father had paid attention to the finer points

of his statue, chipped delicately at the scales, at the fins, determined to make them perfect in every detail, because this was Lou's memorial. Now the light was fading, and he put his tools away, thinking, I'll finish it tomorrow. You'd like it, Lou. It's all for you.

As he gazed at the sinking sun, another wretched day without her coming to an end, he caught sight of something – a dark smudge on the horizon.

He stood still, shading his eyes. Slowly, slowly, it became clear: it was a ship with a big square sail, drawing closer across the darkening water – and there was something in the air ahead of it, a tangled knotty shape.

Winged creatures in a cluster.

Though he couldn't see the ropes, he realized, with horror, that the ship was being towed. And before long he could see what the creatures in the sky were, pulling the vessel by ropes tethered from the bow to their powerful necks...

"DRAGONS!" he cried out in horror and disbelief.

CHAPTER 41

High above the island, crossing the shoreline as
he dragged the boat as far as it would go without
beaching it, Rampant looked down and saw the man.
And knew him, too. He'd kept in his think-space
a pic-tur – rare for dragons who don't tend to back-
think – of this upright as he'd last seen him, running
after him as he flew away with Lou in his jaws,
screaming, "Bring her back! Bring her *back*!"

And now Rampant *was* bringing her back, and he
felt certain that in all his long dragon life, he'd never
felt more conflicted.

The rope tying him to the boat was almost
throttling him and he knew how hard the journey
must have been for the new dragons, whose wings –
though they'd practised flying for many lights and
darks before setting off – were still nothing like as
strong as his. It had been a truly heroic effort on their

part to help him haul this load back to his mainland, never mind stopping off at Lou's island first.

"To show you forgive them," his son had explained.

A lucky wind had blown up to help the dragons over the last stretch of water to the island where Killdragon stood, a tiny figure frozen with disbelief and fear on the beach.

Rampant signalled the others by tilting his wings downward. With faint gurgles of relief, the puller-dragons came to land on the shore, their claws grinding on the pebbled cove.

The boat stopped in deep water, and uprights hastily scrambled about, bringing the big sail down before its vast flapping surface could fill with wind and pull them ashore. An anchor was dropped, and everyone came up on deck, staring at the man on the beach.

He stared back, trying to make sense of it.

Were these dragons coming to attack the island? Surely!

But somehow a dim, mysterious instinct made him doubt it. It was the little red dragon standing up on the prow, gazing at him and nodding as if to reassure him, that gave him a stab of hope. No. More than that. It was a kind of lightening of the spirit.

The red dragon lifted himself into the air. Then, as it wheeled to approach the island, he saw her, sitting astride the red body, hands holding fast to its fin…

"DAD!"

On they came, swooping low so that Red's feet skimmed the curling waves. Lou's excited features became rapidly clearer – and now her father could hear her calling him, just above the rhythmic crashing of waves as he ran to the water's edge to meet her.

The time for thinking, for doubting, for being afraid, was at a sudden end, washed away like the tiny pebbles beneath his feet. Now his whole mind was given over to one feeling: joy. It no longer mattered that she was perched on the back of a dragon. All that mattered was that she was here, returned to him!

He ran, stumbling, and stopped as his bare feet entered the water, jumping up and down and waving wildly with both arms.

"Look! It's him – it's *him* – it's my dad!" Lou shouted to the dragons. "Land! Oh, please land!"

Red tilted his wings slightly into the wind, and gently came in to land. Lou slid off Red's back straight into her father's arms. He held her, eyes tight shut, savouring the moment. Red, thinking it impolite to intrude on the reunion, took off, rising quickly to a safe height.

At last Lou's dag drew away from her, staring at her through wet eyes.

"My girl! My darling girl! You came back!" But then his expression changed to suspicion. "What is this – a miracle? What are you doing here? How did you come?"

"It was Red, Dad," she said, pointing up at her friend hovering expertly above them. Her father glanced, but only for a moment – he wanted to put the sight of the monster out of his mind.

"*Red?*"

She nodded. "He brought me in the ship – him and the others and the uprights – I mean skyscraper people – across the sea. They brought me back."

"Who – those *monsters*?"

The word *monster*, coming from her father, landed like a blow.

"Not monsters, Dad. They're creatures. Like us."

He studied the face that he loved so deeply and had missed so much, and felt something stronger than relief. It was anger creeping into his veins and threatening to destroy his moment of joy. He stood there, staring at her, wondering whether these thieving brutes had done something to her – threatened her, maybe, to bring her on to their side. Anything was possible. They were dragons after all. His response, when it finally came, was terse.

"Dragons are *nothing* like us." He took a step back, and his voice became stern. "I must go back to the village and warn them. Only this time it'll be different."

"Different?"

"This time we're ready. And you're coming with me." He took her hand and gave it a sharp, persuasive tug, but she resisted.

"No, Dad! You've got it all wrong! They're not our enemies any more; they're our friends!"

A sudden rush of wind and the beating of huge wings swallowed up his reply. The next thing he knew he was being roughly nudged by a massive armoured head, which sent him flying backwards onto the pebbles.

It was Rampant.

Thinking this was an attack on Lou, he'd sprung to her rescue, and now that his fire was up and his claws were drawn, the instinct to rip-burn-kill was rushing through him. He towered over the girl's dag, pinning him to the ground with one claw.

"No, Dag! Stop! You're hurting him!" cried Red, swooping down.

The man felt the dragon release him.

For a moment, he didn't dare open his eyes.

Now, as he lay there blinking, he could see them: his daughter, on her knees, stroking his sand-spattered hair tenderly, and the dragons – one massive, the other smaller and distinctly red – staring down at him. Or was it glaring?

"It's all right; you'll be all right now." It was Lou's voice, gentle and calming. "He thought you were hurting me. He was just trying to protect me."

"From what? Your own *father*?"

"It was a mistake," said Red, giving his dag a sharp look. "He didn't mean to scare you. Did you, Dag?"

"No, I didn't mean to—" Rampant stopped himself quickly, and coughed out a little grey smoke, like a bad think dispelled. Then in a more restrained tone he added, "I thought you ... I thought... It doesn't matter."

"You could've killed him!" Lou said reproachfully.

Rampant said nothing. She was right, of course – he *could* have killed the upright. Easily. All it would have taken was a tiny push of a claw against his delicate skin. For some reason, the think deeply unsettled him.

Lou helped her father to sit up, which he did with difficulty, wiping dragon spittle from his face. Finally he managed to get to his feet. He looked at Rampant. For some reason, the fear had left him. Now it was just one father speaking to another.

"You took my daughter. I'd given up hope of ever seeing her again. Do you know what that's like? Have you *any* idea how it feels to think you've lost your only child?"

Rampant remembered the moment when he thought

Red was drowning, and another when he was fighting the shark.

"Yes," he replied gravely. "I know exactly how that feels."

Red looked at his dag. It was something in the full-grown's stance, the way he hung his head in silence, that showed he was feeling – what? Shame? As he stood there, a think came to Red.

For griffilin to happen, dragons and uprights had to understand that skin and scales are only a cover for the same thing. And thinks? Thinks could only get you so far...

Dos might get you all the way.

CHAPTER 42

Rampant looked down at Lou's father.

"I shouldn't have taken her," he said. "It was undragonly." He paused as if struck by a strange realization, and then he turned to his son. "It's all so much easier when you don't actually know your enemy – when you still believe you're better than he is."

The black dragon jumped over to where the others were gathered some distance away on the beach. Red jumped after him.

"And what do you believe now, Dag?"

"That life was a lot easier before I started thinking and feeling so much."

Lou ran over, looking worried. "Dag – Rampant, I mean," she said. "Aren't you going to say goodbye?"

Rampant looked down at her wonderingly. He remembered the first time he'd set eyes on this upright. How weak and vulnerable she'd seemed;

how much she'd grown in his estimation since that day; how much, through her love and her courage and her kindness, *all* uprights had grown. He lowered his head until his eyes were staring directly into hers.

"If I had a she-mumbo, I'd hope she'd grow up to be as clever and brave as you are." And he put his snout down and gave her a gentle little nuzzle. "How can it be goodbye if I keep you in my think-space?"

She looked at him and smiled. "I'll keep you in *my* think-space, too."

It felt suddenly as if the ground beneath his feet were moving. But it was deeper than earth. This was *sorrow* – an unfamiliar feeling strong enough to shake even a fierce giant like him to the core.

Suddenly his pair swooped down as if from nowhere. "We have to go," she said firmly. "The wind's against us. Time is running out."

"Yes," replied Rampant, straightening up and looking more like his old self again.

Lou looked at Perilous – the huge green dragon who'd become, in her own mother's absence, like a mum. No, a *mag*. She ran over to her, flinging her arms round her neck and hugging her tightly.

"I love you, Mag!" she said. "I love you all so very, very much!"

"We ... love you too," said Perilous, surprised at her own feelings, and she patted the little furry upright head with one paw. Lou drew away for a moment, looking up at the full-grown.

"Would you like to say hello to my dad?"

Perilous glanced over at the man standing perfectly still by the water's edge.

"Next time, perhaps."

"Next time?" put in Red excitedly. "You mean we might come back?"

"If I've learned anything on this mission of ours," said his mag, spreading her wings, "it's that anything is possible."

From where Lou's dag was standing, he could see the dragons preparing for take-off. Suddenly he was running – running as fast as he could, waving and shouting words he could never have imagined he'd ever say.

"I forgive you!" he cried. "I FORGIVE YOU!"

Rampant and his pair were already too high to

hear him, but they saw him, and signalled. The other dragons began to rise, straining against the pull of the ropes between their teeth.

Red and Lou stood there on the beach gazing up at the black cloud of dragons moving purposefully across the sky, pulling the great boat laden with coal back out to sea.

"*True hope is swift, and flies with dragons' wings*, as Shakespeare nearly said," Lou whispered under her breath.

They knew they had to say goodbye, but neither could bring themselves to do it. Everything they had been through together had freed them of the Old Time stories. They'd made a new one, a better one, together.

But there could be no more delaying.

Red turned to Lou and found her staring at him through rain-filled eyes.

"Well?" he asked.

"Well," she replied.

There was a moment of silence, and then he jumped closer, and reached out a paw. She gave him her hand. He gazed at it – the fabled hand – the way he'd gazed at it so long ago: not with resentment or fear any more but with awe for what it could cause – such amazing,

beautiful things. All it
took was the right kind
of think-space.

"It's like Dag said;
it's…"

"Not goodbye?"

Red looked over at
Lou's father. "Tell your
dag to tell the others – your
peepuls, I mean – about griffilin. Tell them to help
change the pattern."

"I will. I can't promise they'll listen, but I'll try."

"If dragons can listen," said Red, "peepuls can listen
too."

He'd learned that. And he believed it. And it would
be *that* hope more than any conjured by angels and
ministers that would give him strength for the long
journey home.

Red snorted a puff of white smoke – whiter than
Lou had ever seen before. She knew what it meant.
Peace.

He spread his wings and let them catch the wind
blowing in from the sea. He rose up and up until Lou
and her father were no more than tiny dots on their

island home. Higher he flew to claim his place among the other dragons who, led by his mag and dag, were pulling the big boat. Perilous glanced back, signalling with her tail for him to hurry. He flapped his wings vigorously, and soon caught up.

All the while his think-space was ablaze as any chest-fire with anxious thinks about how they might be received when they arrived home. The Council would surely be happy that they had returned with coal. But brought by uprights, and led to the mainland by none other than their own dragons? Would they think Rampant a traitor, bringing coal, yes, but uprights with it? And yet without upright hands to help them, how could they unload the coal?

Red, as he flew, practised the explanations he'd give. He'd fly fast, get there first, call a heads-together, convince the Council. If those they'd left behind could change, then it was possible that those waiting up ahead could change too. If the hate and mistrust and the dark, fearsome legends of old could be forgotten – *truly* forgotten – then in the name of Flame, *surely* it was possible everywhere, throughout the mainlands and the islands, to spread griffilin.

Griffilin!

Once it had been nothing more than an impossible whisper, the most fragile of thinks. But now it could become real. And it was up to him, the Red Dragon, to bring it about. Feeling the life-giving heat in his chest-fire glowing, and spreading his wings to their fullest extent, he began to draw ahead.

"Angels and ministers of grace," he shouted over the sound of the wind, "and Lou – always Lou!"

Thinking of her as if she were on his back, her knees pressed tightly to his sides and her hands gripping his fin, he flew strongly home.

EPILOGUE

One day, many warms and colds later, visitors from the nearest dragon live-place flew to the popular little island called Haven, which had a reputation for pretty scenery, good cooking, and a friendly welcome from its upright inhabitants.

Though it was a long flight away, it was a favourite place for breaks from the mainland, no longer exclusively inhabited by dragons but by a comfortable mix of the two species, who shared it and all its advantages. There wasn't much left now from the Old Time, but between them, dragons and uprights had found ways to cause a renewal of Old Time trappings and a lot of newly developed ones which benefited them all.

As the visiting dragons circled the coast a little distance from the town-place, one of them, a she-mumbo, swerved away and landed beside something she'd spotted from the air.

Her parents, noticing, followed, and soon they were all standing on the beach, resting their wings and studying the thing that had attracted the youngster's attention.

"Look, Mag! Dag! What is it?" she asked.

"Well, Gentle, you can see what it is. It's a statue of a half-grown and a young she-upright."

"But why's she riding on his back?"

"When you learn to read, you can know. Look, there's a piece of knowledge written underneath it."

"Read it to me, Mag!"

Her mag peered down at the words carved into a wooden plaque set in the ground at the foot of the statue, and read. Dragons could do that now.

> "TO BE, OR NOT TO BE?"
> THAT <u>WAS</u> THE QUESTION.
> UNTIL THEY FOUND THE ANSWER.

"That's from Shakespeare!" squealed Gentle. There was a moment of silence between them. "Can we sing the Red Red Dragon song?" she asked suddenly, "like we do at school?"

Sing it? That was one of many things uprights had taught dragons to do in exchange for some much-needed dragonsense. The three dragons began.

"When the Red Red Dragon comes out of the sky,
I know that I will learn how to fly. When the Red Red
Dragon comes—" Suddenly, other voices broke in, shrill and excited. *"—over the sea, what a day that will*
be for him and for me!"

The dragons turned and saw a full-grown upright and several young ones – also visitors – hurrying towards them. And now they were singing together.

"When the Red Red Dragon comes over the hill,
I know he will come to heal and not kill." Their voices, filled with feeling, rose. *"Red is the colour, Red is the*
name – Red is the dragon that made us the same."

The upright full-grown, a teacher, glanced at the dragons.

"Beautiful monument, isn't it?"

Gentle's mag gave an approving puff of white smoke, and replied, "It's the most beautiful thing that was ever caused."

No one spoke after that. They just stood together, very quietly, letting feelings of deep contentment – dragons had good words for all kinds of emotions now – wash over them, like the sea washing gently over the sand.

And everyone there, dragons and uprights, felt sure that the future, *their* future – once dark and uncertain – was bright; bright like the blaze of light-shine on their skin and their scales; bright like each and every one of their very special think-spaces.

THE BEGINNING